Stories My Mother

Never Told Me

Also by Kenneth Mattern

Fancy: *A story of love and Dementia*

Centerville: *Terror in a small town*

Available at amazon.com

Stories My Mother Never Told Me

Short Stories

By

Kenneth Mattern

Copyright © 2023 by Kenneth Mattern
Cover Art by
starryai

Printed in the United States of America

For information about permission to reproduce selections from this book, write to
Permissions, ESSPC-LLC
9729 Wallwood Dr. SE
Huntsville, AL 35803

ISBN: 979-8-9856640-7-2

Published by Elegant Solutions Software and Publishing Company, LLC.
Copyright ©2023 All Rights Reserved

10 9 8 7 6 5 4 3

For Beth and Seth, I never told them stories
like this

Table of Contents

Stories My Mother Never Told Me

Introduction

Welcome, dear reader, to Stories My Mother Never Told Me. In this volume you will meet friends of mine who have been rambling in my head for many years. Some of them are new friends and some are hoary and old. I can assure that my mother, may she rest in peace, never told me about any of them. And it's probably a good thing that she didn't.

She taught me to be a gentleman, to rise when a lady enters a room, how to eat properly, hold the door for others, and... you get the picture.

She never told me about people like Fred, who you will meet in The Cave, or Sam, the millionaire or the cat herder you will meet in King Boots or any of the other individuals you will surely meet in these pages.

So, *I* will tell you about them and I will tell you their stories. Some of them you might not want to read on a dark night. Others, you will. So, sit back and enjoy.

Stories My Mother Never Told Me

The Last Signal

When I heard, on the news, the theory that NASA had developed as to why we have never received signals from alien civilizations, it both surprised me and saddened me at the same time. Sadly, NASAs theory makes perfect sense. See if you can make out what it is by the time you finish this story.

"**We** have another." Jarrl said as it looked up from his console. "It's out toward the rim but the signals are clear and strong. Maybe this one..."

"Do not count on this. You know the record." Replied Namond, Jarrl's associate. "They never last long. At least this signal makes three, the most we have had on an extremely long time. But the other two are soon to disappear, they are getting to that state."

Jarrl nodded, "I hope that this one is different."

"Hope in one cache and distribute in another and determine which fills first."

Stories My Mother Never Told Me

Jarrl nodded, resigned to what it knew the future of this latest signal was to be. Jarrl was a part of a small AI team that listened for signals from space. Their observatory was above the plane of the galactic ecliptic and as a result was enabled to receive more and clearer interstellar signals than in the general population of systems in the main body of the galaxy. But "more" was a relative figure. More, right now, meant three signal sources. But the question was, as always, how long would they last?

On average the signals lasted for about one hundred universal years. They sprung up quickly and gained strength for a number of years, then steadied off but at a high rate of strength and data. Then they usually disappeared almost as though a switch had been thrown.

Jarrl went about its business monitoring the new signals. It often wished that it could translate the audio signals into thoughts, words or ideas but try as they might, they had no luck. At least music could be entertaining, so to speak. Video signals were better as at least the bureau AIs could "see" what was going on and even, sometimes, interpret what was happening.

Stories My Mother Never Told Me

The bureau, officially the Intelligent Signal Monitoring Bureau, using sophisticated multiple frequency receivers could, in theory, monitor the weakest attenuated signals from up to three hundred universal lightyears distance. But normally all they received was noise.

This newest signal was very strong and originated from the outer rim of the galaxy, it was probably traveling a distance of one or two hundred universal lightyears. Right now, in the early stages as they usually were, simple data streams of short and long signals were received in the low kilohertz frequencies. Jarrl knew that as time passed the signals would move into much higher frequencies and ultimately would become digitized and be broadcast from space rather than the planet's surface. That signals were broadcast from space became apparent as the signal quality suddenly clarified and intensified. Then in the microwave range the data became almost overwhelming. Classifying all that information was almost impossible. It was all digitized and the AI team worked hard to try to gather recognizable data from it. Sadly, it also meant that the signals would not

Stories My Mother Never Told Me

last many years more before they stopped. That was always the case.

Individuals like Jarrl existed for very long periods of time. It could actually exist for a much longer period of time than the longest lasting signals ever received. It had monitored from completion to end, two sets of signals and would probably last well beyond the present new set of signals before it was retired, to be replaced by a new generation of AI monitors. But for much of its time of monitoring for signals from space, it had heard nothing. So now was a busy time.

Then, sometime after the new signal was received the oldest of the other two signals suddenly ended. They always ended suddenly. Usually, it was presaged by a rather strong signal of pure energy, some of which was in within the monitored frequencies and then nothing. As was the case this time.

And now there were two.

* * * * *

It was Marconi who generated the first radio signals in 1895. It was the basis of what would

Stories My Mother Never Told Me

become wireless telegraphy – the sending of Morse Code signals over the air using radio signals. The early versions simply turned on and off the "transmitter" producing dots and dashes of electrical energy in the form of radio waves. These primitive signals would only propagate for perhaps half a mile. Then Marconi developed the method of raising the height of his antenna and grounding the transmitter which enabled him to send signals up to three miles. Within a few short years wireless radio was born.

By the 1920s commercial radio was introduced and became the main form of entertainment in most households. By the 1950s Very High Frequency (VHF) stations began broadcasting and at about the same time television was developed and coming into people's homes.

By the turn of the twenty-first century digital radio signals were being broadcast via satellite and satellites were routinely transmitting radio, video and data signals worldwide – and beyond. Of course, satellite broadcasting had been in use for quite some time.

Stories My Mother Never Told Me

Arthur C. Clarke was the first to predict the concept of satellite communication back in October, 1945 in the Wireless World journal. In it he wrote:

"ALTHOUGH it is possible, by a suitable choice of frequencies and routes, to provide telephony circuits between any two points or regions of the earth for a large part of the time, long-distance communication is greatly hampered by the peculiarities of the ionosphere, and there are even occasions when it may be impossible. A true broadcast service, giving constant field strength at all times over the whole globe would be invaluable, not to say indispensable, in a world society...

It will be possible in a few more years to build radio controlled rockets which can be steered into such orbits beyond the limits of the atmosphere and left to broadcast scientific information back to the earth. A little later, manned rockets will be able to make similar flights with sufficient excess power to break the orbit and return to earth."

On June 10th, 1962 the company AT&T launched Telstar 1, the world's first active

9

Stories My Mother Never Told Me

telecommunications satellite and everything changed. By the turn of the century people were listening to "satellite radio" and television was broadcast worldwide. Data streamed into space at a prodigious rate and the earth fairly screamed at the stars.

The first atomic bomb exploded on July 16, 1945. Ten years later the earth was in a position where the two major powers and a couple of other countries had developed enough nuclear weapons to destroy the world many times over; they developed a term for that - Mutually Assured Destruction (MAD), it was coined with the understanding that if one side launched a nuclear attack and the other side responded in kind, the result would be that the entire world would be blasted back into the stone ages. This was the cold war and despite historical assurances, it never ended.

In the first quarter of the twenty first century, only a hundred thirty years after Marconi's invention of radio, the threat of nuclear war raised its head once again. And this time it was serious.

* * * * *

Stories My Mother Never Told Me

The signal ended and Jarrl silently mourned in its own way. It knew that, once again, a civilization had ended in nuclear war. The fatal signature of the Electro Magnetic Pulse (EMP) was the final and loud crashing of the planet's radio emissions as its populations were destroyed.

And now there were two.

The new signal was growing in strength and some parts of the signal were becoming more discrete. The video signals were especially strong. Jarrl enjoyed watching one set off videos which claimed, "I Love Lucy." Of course, it couldn't decipher this but it enjoyed the antics of the moving characters and the sounds they emitted.

It was at this same time that the second signal ceased. The symptoms and signals were the same. Jarrl easily recognized the ending EMP and again it paused to mourn the passing of another intelligent species.

And now there was one.

It had been hypothesized the reason that there had never been actual contact and communication between alien races is that they had

Stories My Mother Never Told Me

all developed their civilizations to the point where they destroyed themselves in wars – nuclear wars. That these civilizations could not even begin to fathom how to create a lasting peace or, at least, a non-belligerent co-existence seemed to be impossible.

And so it went.

Jarrl monitored the last signal. Lucy disappeared and other broadcasts came into being. There were strange events, perhaps practice for war, where crowds of individuals gathered to observe two opposing entities brutally battle over a small oblong object. But at least nobody died.

Then there was music. Jarrl like the music, especially the hard beats and rhythms. Classical it found boring. And it discovered what appeared to be millions of brief educational video programs centered on reproduction. Jarrl assumed that this must be something difficult to learn. It just wished that it could understand the audio that accompanied these video lessons. But they, for the most part, appeared to be some non-verbal form of communication.

Stories My Mother Never Told Me

The most disturbing, though, were those that depicted real combat. There was no mistaking that. And Jarrl knew that war had most definitely come to this place. It didn't know how advanced war making had become on this planet. There was, after all, only so much that could be learned from these broadcasts.

And then, in a short time, the finality of the EMP was observed and all was quiet.

Once again Jarl listened and watched but it would be five hundred universal years before it detected another signal.

Until then, it was once more alone.

Stories My Mother Never Told Me

Kevlar

UFOs, or now they are called UAPs by the government, have long been a subject of fascination. Many believe that they are extraterrestrial in origin while others believe they are purely earthly. No matter what you currently believe, you may change your mind after reading this story.

"I'm Your Grandson," Alien Says

DATELINE MARSHALL SPACE FLIGHT CENTER: In an exclusive release to Wierdly World News, Mr. Bob "Buzz" Hotckiss, the head of the Extraterrestrial Office of NASAs Marshall Space Flight Center in Huntsville, Alabama, revealed that aliens aren't aliens after all. Mr. Hotckiss granted an exclusive interview with his top-secret resident "alien".

"I'm not from outer space," said Kevlar the 'alien', "I'm from Nebraska. It's impossible to travel any interstellar distance in anything close to an ordinary lifetime. As a matter of fact," he continued, "I'm from your future; from the year 2525. Despite

Stories My Mother Never Told Me

the Iran, Israel nuclear war of 2024 man does still survive."

Kevlar who only uses a first name, because the world population is so small that everybody knows everybody, continued by talking about the world devastation caused by the nuclear conflict. According to him the entire world was almost bombed out of existence. He also stated that his world is rapidly dying.

Kevlar resembles the classic "Gray" alien, but on close inspection he wears dark wraparound sunglasses because the sunlight in our current era is too strong for his eyes. He is also only five feet tall and weighs about eighty pounds. "It's the diet we have to live on," he said.

When asked why people from his time are invading our time, he denied that it was an invasion. "We need you so very badly," he calmly stated. "Our DNA is almost completely destroyed and if we don't find a solution soon, we will all die. Humanity will be gone."

He explained that his group of people in the future Nebraska had learned the secret of time travel. What they are apparently doing is returning

Stories My Mother Never Told Me

to our present time, before the war in 24 in order to locate their ancestors.

What *we* think of as alien abductions are actually "sampling missions" as Kevlar called them. "We don't abduct anyone. They all wake up in their own beds just a little worse for wear. We don't hurt our ancestors, our grandparents, in any way. We simply need samples."

According to Kevlar by locating ancestors, true blood relatives, his teams can retrieve samples of flesh and DNA in hopes of replicating both in the year 2525. By doing so they hope to replace their dying DNA with the fresh and clean DNA from their pre nuclear war ancestors. He said that the samples of flesh are taken in hopes of culturing it in order to rebuild lost muscles in their own bodies.

"We're not here to hurt anybody," he said. "We just need help. If you see us please do not be afraid. Instead welcome us with open arms. Give us a pound of flesh and a little DNA. After all you are doing it for your grandchildren."

Kevlar said that it was impossible to alter the past which is why the war will take place in 2024.

Stories My Mother Never Told Me

"We can't do it," he said. "If only we could," he said wistfully. "If only we could."

Stories My Mother Never Told Me

The Cave

If you read my book Centerville, and I hope you do, you will meet the characters in this story. But this story does not fit into the account told of Centerville. But the characters are all in character, so to speak. Both the good and the bad.

Of course, the Dry Run wasn't really dry. Most of the year, it ran anything from a trickle to a moderately flowing stream. It flowed down behind the village of Centerville. Snaking along the side of a hill and down past the long-crumbled lime kiln that once stood in a cut in the very same hill. Near the lime kiln it split into two to flow around an island. On the field side, to the west, it filled a nice sized pool that often had suckers to catch as well as sunfish and rock bass. On the hill side it disappeared into the earth.

In years past men had put red dye into the stream at that spot and found it flowing into the Cave Creek a good three-quarters of a mile away. At that spot in the Cave Creek a spring flowed into the river; Cave Creek was too wide and deep to really be called a creek, despite its name. The morning after

Stories My Mother Never Told Me

the dye had been poured into the hole in the Dry Run at the lime kiln, the spring, which emerged at the base of a huge oak tree, flowed red for a number of hours.

After the dye experiment, they tried digging open the hole where the Dry Run disappeared but were unable to make progress of any kind. They tried dynamite, also to no avail. Dispirited the group finally gave up hopes of opening a cave and commercializing it.

And there *was* a cave, no doubt about that. From that point by the lime kiln to the point of the spring entering Cave Creek, which was almost a straight line, with a jog near the end, things had happened. A sink hole at least twenty feet deep had opened up in the field of a farm along that line. Not much more than five hundred feet away, closer to the creek, a stream running behind the farmer's house partially flowed into a pool that drained into the earth. The farmer dug at that hole and, at one point, pried with a six-foot crowbar. The crowbar slipped from his hands and disappeared into the earth completely. He also had no luck excavating the hole into the cave.

Stories My Mother Never Told Me

Further along the line, a geologist doing a survey, said that a fault ran along the believed path of the cave for about a quarter mile. And only about eight hundred feet from the spring entering the Cave Creek a well driller noted that at one point, approximately fifty feet below the entry point the drill bit dropped about fifteen to twenty feet – trough a cavity. The drill bit came to a stop at about the same level as the nearby spring, as well as the same approximate level where the crowbar went underground.

Everyone knew that there was a cave along that line.

In the time of Jimmy Harris and Ben Snyder, say the summer of 1957, the cave was an unknown known entity. Unknown, because nobody really knew anything about it except that all evidence pointed to its existence. *Known* because everybody knew that there had to be a cave there because *all the evidence pointed to its existence.*

That is until early June of 1957. For a few days the Dry Run wasn't. It started with a series of storms that brewed between Lewistown and State College. It was between these two small cities that

Stories My Mother Never Told Me

large storms formed and were channelled by the mountains. The Seven Mountains were like a hand with the fingers spreading wide on the western end and funnelling, some thirty-five miles to the east, to the area between Port Mifflin and Middlebury. The paths included Port Mifflin itself, Bald Eagle Mountain to its north, Cave Creek to the south, Johns Mountain, south of the river, Centerville on the south side of Johns Mountain along with Middlebury, and Shade Mountain to that town's south. A total distance of of eleven and a half miles, north to south.

It could rain along Cave Creek and just across the bridge heading to Centerville a quarter mile away there would be a straight line across the road. One side wet and the other dry.

One particular set of storms brewed up to the west and followed Johns Mountain, inundating all the area between Burnam and Centerville. It rained for three days solid. The Dry Run belied its name and ran full. There was so much water that the stream changed its course just east of Centerville. It scrubbed the island at the lime kiln and formed a pool that emptied into a newly formed whirlpool

Stories My Mother Never Told Me

where the stream drained into the cave. And it drained for over a week.

The day after the rain stopped Jimmy Harris and Ben Snyder walked along the stream's bank to see what they might discover in the newly washed fields and banks. It was prime arrow head hunting time, where the artifacts would be lifted from the mud and washed clean. The boys had found many in the past summer or two just by hunting after a heavy rain. And today was no different. Ben, who had the better eyesight for things like this, found a nice point. Later Jimmy spied a piece of flat stone that looked like it had been worked by Indians. As they examined the artifact, the boys agreed that it was probably a part of a larger knife blade. They could see where the stone had been worked to fit a human hand with spots smoothed out for thumbs and fingers. It had been long thought that that an Indian village had occupied that spot

As they approached the lime kiln, they could see that the wider and deeper part of the stream had formed to the left of the island while a good amount of water still flowed the other way and was pooling at point where it normally drained into the cave. When they approached that spot Jimmy pointed and

Stories My Mother Never Told Me

said, "Do you see that? And can you hear it bubbling?"

"I can see it all right and it almost sounds like flushing the toilet."

The boys came closer and stood in awe as they watched the thick looking muddy water swirling around in a circle and then disappearing into the ground. It *did* kind of sound like a flushing toilet.

"Man, I wonder how many gallons are going down there and where it's going." Ben said.

"It's going into the cave!" Jimmy exclaimed. "I wonder how big the drain hole will be when it runs out of water."

"With this much water it probably won't stop for another day or so," said Ben. "I remember my grandmother telling me how her father and some other men actually blasted with dynamite and everything, trying to open a cave entrance here. They completely failed. Gramma also said that he dumped red dye into the hole here and it came out in Cave Creek the next day. I wonder how big the cave is. I'd love to get into it and explore it."

Stories My Mother Never Told Me

"Well, maybe in a couple of days we can see whether the opening has been made bigger. Maybe we can get into it. If we do I wonder what we'll find."

"I think we'll find a lot of mud. That's what I think," Ben nodded at the whirlpool.

"Maybe, but I think we'll find smooth and clean stone. This water is moving so quickly that there will be mud only in pools underground but not the floor and walls." Jimmy was imagining a cave with flat gravelled floors and smooth curved walls that met overhead, like what he had seen last summer at Windwood cave that he and his family had toured while at family reunion. Windwood cave was the closest commercial cave and the only one Jimmy had ever seen.

Ben had never been underground.

They returned every day to check the level of the water there at the lime kiln. And the water was slowly receding but the whirlpool was still just as strong as the previous day. And it was the same for four days. On the fifth day the water was suddenly only a trickle and the boys could see that the hole in the streambed was open and led into darkness. In fact it was well over a foot across. There were a

Stories My Mother Never Told Me

number of loose smallish boulders around the edge as well as a lot of loose gravel. Jimmy thought that the rush of water forced all the smaller stuff into the hole and he was right.

They examined the hole closely. Jimmy took from his knapsack a three-cell flashlight that he always carried in the pack. He knelt by the raindrop shaped hole and turned on the flashlight. He pointed it into the hole and saw nothing. The beam of light was engulfed by the darkness.

"It's deep," he said.

Ben dropped a pebble into the hole and they waited for what seemed to be an eternity before they heard a splash far below. In actuality they waited less than a second but as Einstein said, time is relative.

"It *is* deep," Ben breathed.

"Drop in another and we'll count one-one thousand as it falls to figure out how deep it really is."

Ben did so and they each got to 'one-one thousand one, one-thou' before they heard the stone splash in the water.

Stories My Mother Never Told Me

"Didja hear the echo?" Ben asked. "It sounds like it fell into a big room."

"Yeah, and the floor is about 20, 25 feet down! That's quite a ways. Farther than I expected."

"How do you know that?"

"Things speed up in freefall at an approximate rate of thirty-two feet per second, per second." Jimmy sagely said.

"What? That doesn't make any sense. What does that mean?"

Jimmy tried again, "If you drop a stone from the roof of your house it will fall about sixteen feet in the first second. You would think that it will fall thirty-two feet in the second second. But it will actually fall closer to sixty-four feet. That's because it keeps going faster at a rate of thirty-two feet per second, for every second it falls. I know that it's complicated and I barely understand it at all. Just trust me that the hole is about twenty feet or so deep."

"I gotta trust you. I know you know shit like this but I don't know how you know it." Ben sighed.

Stories My Mother Never Told Me

"I just like to think and learn about stuff like this. One day I want to be a science teacher, so I have to get a head start."

"I hope I'm never in your class," Ben teased. "But this isn't getting us any closer to the water that must be at the bottom of the hole. Say, what if we tie a string around the flashlight and lower it down the hole. Think we'll see anything?"

"Maybe. Let's try it. I have a ball of string in my pack."

"Of course, you do." Ben teased. "It's just like The Batman's Utility Belt. It holds *everything*!"

"Not quite," Jimmy smiled as he pulled the ball of string from his pack. He quickly tied the end to the loop at the base end of the flashlight. It was an Army type that made a bend at the light end so you actually held the light upright to see ahead.

When he finished, he knelt by the hole. He unwound some string and gave the ball to Ben, "Hang onto it. We don't want it to go down the hole."

Ben did hold onto it as he peered into the hole along with Jimmy, their noses almost below the surface of the still slowly flowing stream. The knees

Stories My Mother Never Told Me

of their pants got soaked in the water of the stream but they never noticed. The light slowly spun on its axis as they lowered it. At first, they could see nothing as they carefully unwound the string. But soon, as it spun, they could see glimpses of walls.

"Damn, I should have tied knots in the string every foot or so, so we can tell how deep it is."

"It's not that far down. Let's pull it up and do it," replied Ben. And so, they did. Jimmy knew that his outstretched hand extending from thumb to middle finger was almost exactly six inches, so he guessed the length of a foot and broke a nearby twig to that length. Then, using the stick as a ruler, they tied knots based on the stick's length.

Once again, they lowered the flashlight. This time they counted the knots. At four knots they saw the walls and at eight knots the walls faded into darkness. They saw nothing until the flashlight reached the water.

"Hope it's waterproof," said Ben.

"It's supposed to be." The flashlight hung above the water but the boys couldn't really see much of anything except the light flashing off the

Stories My Mother Never Told Me

water once in a while as it spun in the darkness. After a short time, Jimmy pulled the light back to the surface. They stood up and noticed their wet knees.

Looking around Ben said, "You know. I think we should try damming the run up there." He pointed to a spot upstream where it looked like they could divert the water away from the hole. "If it works, we could get this place pretty dry. Then we could dig away the loose stones and see if we can move some of those bigger rocks. I can get dad's crowbar and maybe we can get down into the cave."

"Maybe we could," Jimmy agreed. "But we would need at least a strong rope. And more light. And," being the practical one, "we need to be really careful. I don't want to fall into that hole and get stuck. The other thing is that we don't want Fred to discover what we're doing. He comes down here often enough and I don't want him snooping around our worksite."

Ben nodded in agreement.

What the boys didn't know was that Fred was indeed watching them at this very moment. Huddled in his fort made of straw bales in the hay mow of

Stories My Mother Never Told Me

McMaster's barn which overlooked the field leading to the lime kiln.

Fred Swartz was the local bully. He was only fourteen but he terrorized the younger children in the village. Sometimes he actually physically intimidated them and beat a few of them over time. Many openly feared him. He wasn't as much of a bully to the larger boys and even played basketball and baseball with them on occasion. He had fished at the lime kiln with both Jimmy and Ben. Sometimes he was nice but most times he wasn't.

Fred was a wanderer. His mother was confined to a wheel chair and so he became pretty independent. In fact, when school was not in session, he was rarely in his own home. He often would go camping, along the Dry Run or along Cave Creek, for days at a time. He'd take a little cooking gear, fishing rod and his .22 rifle and would catch, shoot or steal his food and cook it over his camp fire.

'I wonder what they're up to.' He thought to himself. He knew that the stream did drain through a smallish hole in the streambed. 'Are they digging at the hole? Are they trying to get into the cave? That would be fun to explore.' He continued to watch as

Stories My Mother Never Told Me

Jimmy and Ben began to build the stream diverting dam.

The boys walked about fifty feet upstream and began to scrounge for rocks large enough to build the dam. Their pants soon were completely soaked. In the early afternoon June heat, they took off their shirts and began to sweat in the hot sun. After about an hour their dam was beginning to take shape. Water was slowly being diverted.

"I think we should put some small branches against the upstream side of the dam and maybe push some mud against them. That would really block the water." Ben, the budding engineer said.

Jimmy nodded at this idea. They continued to lay out the shape of the dam. In another hour it was high and long enough to make them think it would actually work. Then they began to gather loose branches, many already torn from their parent trees in the flood, and lay them against the upstream side as Ben had suggested. The flowing water immediately pressed the branches against the dam and appreciably slowed the flow of water through it.

"That was an excellent idea," said Jimmy. Ben was, after all, the more practical of the two. Sure,

Stories My Mother Never Told Me

Jimmy could talk about how fast a stone would fall but it was Ben who figured out how to actually do things. They worked for another hour and then, hot and tired, they decided to stop for the day. They walked back to the hole in the streambed and could see that the water had almost stopped flowing.

"Another hour or so and we should have all the water blocked," said Ben. Jimmy agreed as they went to retrieve their shirts and then crossed the field and returned to their homes. As each boy encountered his respective mother upon arriving home they were challenged on their wet pants. Both said that they had been playing and digging in the stream. And that was that.

As soon as the boys had left the field and entered the alley Fred rose from his fort and climbed down to the barn floor and went out into the field. He quickly crossed the field and came upon Jimmy's and Ben's excavation. He nodded at the good work they had done almost as though approving. He walked up to the dam and noted how well it too was built. 'I'd have never thought of the trees and mud', he thought.

Stories My Mother Never Told Me

After puttering around for a few more minutes he left. 'Let them do all the work,' he thought. 'If they actually get into the cave, then I'll go down too when they aren't there.' He wanted to see what was under the earth as much as the boys.

'I hope it's big,' he thought as he went back to the barn.

The next day Jimmy and Ben were back at work and within a couple of hours finished the dam. By then the water had completely stopped flowing into the dig, as Ben began to call it. In fact, the redirection of the stream formed a small island as it flowed around a small mound of earth and met back up with the rest of the Dry Run. Engineering at its best.

By early afternoon they came to the conclusion that they should start digging the next day. The examined the teardrop shaped hole and removed some of the smaller loose stones. They knew they would have to pry at the larger ones but truly believed that with a little more work they could actually open the hole wide enough for them to lower themselves into the cavity.

33

Stories My Mother Never Told Me

"I hope it's as big as it sounds," said Jimmy. "With everything I have heard there has to be a cave here that runs all the way to Cave Creek. So, it must be big."

Ben agreed, "Yeah, the echo down there sounds like it's a large room. I just hope the water isn't too deep. Dad has a good long rope in the garage. I think if we tie big knots into it we should be able to climb down and back up. What do you think?"

"That would probably work. We could tie it to that stump next to the hole. And we've climbed that stupid rope in school enough times. I guess we could easily climb down and up. We should have enough light, though. I've been thinking about that. Do you have a flashlight?"

"Yep, we have a five cell at home and extra batteries. How about you."

Jimmy said, "I have that three-cell army flashlight in my pack and some extra batteries too. Do you think we will need to tie the end of the ball of string to something to keep us from getting lost down there?"

Stories My Mother Never Told Me

"Hmmm," Ben thought out loud, "that might be a good idea. How long is the string?"

"Oh I don't know. Probably a hundred feet or so." It was actually only about thirty feet but they didn't know that.

"Ok," Ben said, "Let's call it a day and come back tomorrow morning and see if we can open the dig and then go down." Jimmy nodded in agreement as they peered down into the darkness, their hearts beating a little fast in anticipation of the adventure awaiting them. And adventurous it would be.

Again, the next morning, they were at their task. They found that it was rather easy, with the two of them tugging on the crowbar that the larger of the rocks were pulled out of their sockets without too much effort. They managed to get three of the larger rocks completely out of the hole and onto the ground nearby. But one larger rock fell into the hole and they could hear it crash in the darkness below. The echo seemed to reverberate for a long time.

The time finally came when the hole was a good two by two feet or even a little larger. It was definitely large enough to permit a boy to go through without having to squeeze or hunch the shoulders.

Stories My Mother Never Told Me

"Let's do it," Ben said

They looped the rope, already knotted, around the tree stump and threw the balance into the hole. They put the flashlights into Jimmy's pack which he slung over his shoulder. Jimmy, suddenly, was very nervous. He was afraid of heights and this was no exception. But he wasn't as afraid as he might have been. Subconsciously the descent into the darkness, where he could not actually see into the depths, made the climb feel not as dangerous. And so he took hold of the rope and began to lower himself into the hole. He climbed down slowly and carefully. Feeling carefully for each knot with his feet before moving his hands over the knot they were grasping, he continued down into the darkness. It took him only a few moments to reach the floor of the cave. Once there he immediately took his flashlight from his pack and turned it on.

Shining the light around himself he saw that he was in a room at least twenty or thirty feet wide and about fifteen feet high where the ceiling narrowed to the hole he had just crossed through. The flashlight barely cast enough light into the downstream end of the room that he wasn't sure he could see anything. Upstream he could see the roof

Stories My Mother Never Told Me

and walls narrow to a crawl way that had a little water trickling through it.

"What did you find?" Ben's voice echoed into the room from the earth above. "Can I come down?"

Momentarily startled, Jimmy looked up and shouted, "Yes, come on down."

Ben immediately grasped the rope and made a quick descent. Heights didn't bother him at all and so he quickly stepped onto the floor and splashed the water. Jimmy gave him the five cell and they began their exploration.

As they played their lights onto the walls, they could see that they were not smooth but instead were covered with flowstone. In one small grotto they could see small stalactites growing from the ceiling and smaller stalagmites growing up from the floor to meet them. The calcite glistened in the light and looked like crystals flashing as their flashlights moved over them.

They explored the room thoroughly, getting a little muddy in the process but Jimmy was right, most of the walls and floor were washed clean of mud. They went deeper into the room, going

Stories My Mother Never Told Me

downstream, discovering new wonders as they walked. Here was a column that grew from the floor and rose to meet the ceiling some fifteen feet overhead.

The boys whispered in awe at what they saw as if talking out loud would disturb the beauty of the place. It was a natural instinct that most people would follow. Once they turned and could see the dim light flowing down through the hole to the surface, a good landmark in the darkness.

All the while they were working, Fred was observing. He thought that it was excellent that they would do all the work for him. As he squatted in his fort in McMaster's hay mow and saw them climb down the rope, he began to get ideas.

In his heart Fred was a very cruel person. Unknown to anybody he had killed a schoolmate just a couple of weeks back, on the Memorial Day holiday, on the last day of school. He threw the body down into a well and nobody had found it. The whole town believed that Patsy Marks had run away from home and Fred, of course, *outwardly* thought the same thing. He didn't know why he got aroused when he did things like that, but he did. Whenever

Stories My Mother Never Told Me

he shot a dog or cat, which he did whenever he thought he could get away with it, he got an erection.

He was getting an erection now and decided to act.

Fred Swope climbed down from the fort and left the barn. He walked calmly across the field to where the boys had disappeared into the earth. He lifted the rope loop from around the tree stump and unceremoniously threw it into the hole.

"Good bye, boys," he said as he walked back to his fort. "See you in hell."

Meanwhile Ben and Jimmy explored deeper into the cave. They quickly realized that it was much more expansive than they had expected. In fact, there were numerous side passages, some looking quite large. "Does it go?" Jimmy wondered out loud, echoing the words many cavers said as they encountered a new passage in their more organized expeditions.

"And, of so, how far," Ben replied. But by unspoken choice they decided to stick to the main passage which still continued to maintain its dimensions the deeper they went into the earth.

Stories My Mother Never Told Me

They did explore some side passages and often stopped to admire formations and flowstone draping the walls. In one place they saw what is commonly called bacon strip; a thin flow of stone, only a fraction of an inch thick and maybe growing as much as a foot down from the ceiling. Shining a light on one side revealed the look of bacon as the light passed through the stone.

Jimmy looked at his watch and exclaimed, "Oh no, Ben, we've been here almost four hours. Mom will be wondering where we're at. We had better go back. We can come again tomorrow." So they turned and retraced their steps, which were really only a couple of hundred feet from the entrance. But when they got there, they found the rope coiled neatly into a pile and none of it led to the surface.

"What the fuck!" Ben shouted. "What happened? How did that get down here?"

"I don't know," Jimmy wailed. "But how can we possibly get out?"

Then he calmed a bit. "I'm sure one of our moms knows we're down here. She won't know what

Stories My Mother Never Told Me

we are doing but maybe they'll look here when we don't come home."

"I sure hope so," Ben shivered. "Maybe if we holler someone will hear us."

And so, they made a godawful noise, shouting for help up through the hole. But the sound didn't go very far once it reached the surface, so they shouted in vain.

And the afternoon passed. As they waited and hoped for rescue, they wandered around the room never far from the light from above.

When Jimmy didn't come home in the afternoon his mother, Carol, began to wonder where he was. 'Probably at Ben's', she thought. While Ben's mother, Janet, Jan to her friends, began to wonder the same thing about her son. 'Probably at Jimmy's' she thought. So, neither gave much thought to her son's location; secure that he was safe with his friend.

Safe they were, for the moment, but they began to chill in the cooler air. The temperature in the cave wasn't much above fifty degrees and the humidity was high, so they began to shiver in the

Stories My Mother Never Told Me

darkness. They flapped their arms and danced in little circles to keep warm.

Meanwhile Fred had returned to his fort and watched intently to see what would happen next. He figured that they probably would get rescued and would be forbidden to enter the cave again, leaving it open to him alone. Just what he wanted – a new hideout.

At five o'clock, after he closed the post office, Ned Harris walked the short quarter mile home. By then Carol was getting a bit concerned and told her husband that Jimmy hadn't been seen since early morning. "Call Jan and ask if he's there?" he replied. Carol went to the phone and called, finally, Jan Snyder. She answered on the first ring.

"Is jimmy down there?" Carol asked. "I haven't seen him since this morning. Is he there?"

"No," Jan answered. After a pause she said, "I thought that Ben was up there with Jimmy. Last I saw of them they were digging, or something, down by the lime kiln."

Stories My Mother Never Told Me

Carol turned to Ned and told him that. He nodded and said, "I'll walk down there and see what I can find."

Carol turned her attention back to her telephone call and said, "Ned is going to the kiln now to see if he can find out if they are there. Maybe they got interested in what they were doing and forgot the time."

"I hope so, but Ben rarely is late when it gets close to supper."

In five minutes, Ned arrived at the lime kiln and immediately found the hole. He knelt and looked into the darkness. He shouted, "Hello! You boys down there?"

Immediately Jimmy and Ben jumped to their feet and Jimmy shouted. "Yes, we're down here, dad. Something happened to our rope and we can't get out!"

'What in hell are they doing down there in the first place? At least they're safe,' he thought. Aloud he shouted, "I'll get Ben's dad and we'll find a way to get you out. Are you ok?"

Stories My Mother Never Told Me

"We're a little chilly but ok. Maybe a little hungry."

"Stay here," Ned shouted needlessly, "I'll be right back." He left and walked across the field to Ben Snyder Sr.'s house and knocked on the back door. Friends never used the front door.

Janice answered and immediately hugged Ned. "Have you found them?"

Ned returned the hug and said, "Yes. They got themselves stuck in a hole in the ground and lost their rope. Ben and I can take a rope or ladder down there and will get them out in no time. How soon will he be home?"

"He should be home any second. Why don't you have a seat in the kitchen till he comes?" She pointed to the kitchen table. "Coffee?" She said and Ned nodded.

"Jan, Can I use the phone to call Carol?" Ben's mother nodded and Ned crossed the kitchen to the telephone and dialed his home.

Carol answered on the first ring, "Well?" she exclaimed.

Stories My Mother Never Told Me

"The boys are fine." Ned said. "They dug a hole in the ground and can't get out. They said something happened to their climbing rope. Ben and I'll have them out in no time."

"But what were they doing? Digging around there?"

"I don't know, yet. But I'll surely find out. They are boys, you know. They do things. The important thing is that they are ok. I'll call later."

Ned didn't have long to wait until Ben got home. He had a job delivering merchandise from the railroad station in Port Mifflin, to various merchants and usually was home in the afternoon. Ben Sr. came clomping into the kitchen and saw Ned sitting at his own table.

"What brings you down here, Ned?"

Ned looked up and said, "Well, Jimmy and Ben Jr. dug themselves into a bit of a hole and need help."

"What do you mean?"

"I mean that they literally dug a hole in the ground down at the lime kiln and climbed down into it. They had a rope but it must have fallen down into the hole after them. Do you have a good rope we can use to get them out?"

"What the hell do they think they were doing?" Ben almost shouted. Jan quivered.

Ned raised his hand, palm forward. "They're boys, Ben. Let's go rescue them first. Then we can think about what they were doing and why. Let's make sure they are safe."

Calmed, Ben Sr. agreed and said, "I got a fifty-foot rope in the barn. Let's get that and the boys."

Within ten minutes the men were at the hole, peering into the darkness. "You boys still there?" Ben Sr. uselessly shouted."

"Of course we are, Dad." Ben Jr. Responded.

"What in hell do you think you were doing?"

Before the boys could answer Ned said, "Let's get them out and then we'll worry about that. I told you once."

"We're lowering down a rope to bring you back up," shouted Ned.

Stories My Mother Never Told Me

"Ok", Jimmy replied, "but you don't need to shout."

Ned played out the rope as Ben Sr. fed it to him. When it reached the boys, Jimmy called upwards. "We'll tie our rope to the end of yours. Loop it over the stump and we can climb up that one." Then he tied the loop of their rope to the end of the other and tugged on the dangling one. "Pull it up!" he called.

Ned pulled the rope back out of the hole and when the loop of the boy's rope came to the sunlight and Ben Sr. untied it and looped it again around the stump. 'Wonder how that came loose,' he thought. It's on there really well.'

"It's secured but tie this rope around your waist while you climb back out," Ben Sr. called down into the dark hole. They boys did so and climbed out of the hole. As each boy came to the surface his father held him tightly to his chest.

The boys sat on the ground and enjoyed the warm late afternoon sunlight. Ben Sr. Began again, "What the fuck did you think you were doing?"

Stories My Mother Never Told Me

Both boys were taken aback at the man's language. They had never heard him talk like that. They looked at the ground and their feet for a while, and then Jimmy said, "There's a big cave down there! We found the hole and just opened it a little bit so we could see what it looks like. It's beautiful and really big. You could open it and people would pay to get in there."

"Not on your life!" said Ben Sr. "We'll fill it up and that will be that."

"But," Ben Jr. blurted, "You really need to see it. It's beautiful."

"Beautiful it may be, but it still has to be blocked off. I don't want you or any other kid falling down there, Why the fall itself would be enough to kill you. Nope that's the way it's got to be."

"We were your age once," Ned said, "And I believe we would probably have done the same thing you did. Boys your age like to do things like that and I'm sure your dad would have been like that too." Reluctantly Ben Sr. Nodded. "It's an adventure, we know, but you have to realize that enterprises like these have consequences. And it'll cost us good money to fill this hole."

Stories My Mother Never Told Me

"No, I don't think *that'll* be hard at all," said a much calmer Ben Sr. "I filled in the well in the back yard last year and I still have the concrete slab that covered it. Must weigh close to a half ton. We can drag it down there tomorrow, behind my truck, and pull it over the hole. No one will get in with that in place. Let's just get the hell out of here."

The men and their sons walked back to their homes. What discussions may have followed are *not* part of this story.

Of course, Fred saw all of the action at the hole and was sorry that there was no violent ending. He had been hoping for at least a good beating. He couldn't hear about the morrow's plans so, of course, he made his own.

In the morning, around eight o'clock, he took a good flashlight and extra batteries and climbed down into the earth using the very same rope that he had unloosed from the stump the day before. While exploring the cave he went deeper and saw more wonderful things than Jimmy and Ben had seen. After all Fred was braver. He wasn't worried at all. And it was the most beautiful thing that Fred had ever seen. He lost track of time, a common occurrence when exploring caves.

Around ten that morning Ben Sr., Ned and the boys dragged the huge slab of concrete down through the field. When they got there, they began to pull it over the hole. Ben Jr. pulled the rope from the stump and threw it into the hole. 'Good riddance,' he thought, remembering the admonishments of the previous evening. One might say that he got whipped a bit. And then he helped the others pull the slab over the hole until it was totally covered. There was no way that anyone could get in – or out.

Fred wasn't missed for almost two weeks.

Stories My Mother Never Told Me

The Old Man and the Kite

I was sitting on the National Seashore beach near Pensacola, Florida enjoying my book, the sea and the wonderful weather. As I read, I watched a father and son assemble a kite and try to fly it. I watched them try to get it into the air and I knew, from my own experience, what the problem was. I should have gone to help – but I didn't.

The day was lovely. Nary a cloud with a nice but intermittent breeze. Down on the beach it was sporadic but above the dunes the wind was steady from the west. The temperature was in the low 80s but with the breeze it felt cooler, of course. The beach itself was nearly deserted with a few people sprinkled up and down the sand, the tassels on their umbrellas bouncing in the air.

The water was warm on this mid-October day. Some men were fishing in the surf, catching little while children were playing in the waves or building sand castles. Other people were swimming out beyond the surf in the waist deep water. A couple of surfers were hoping to find *the* wave, with a little

51

Stories My Mother Never Told Me

luck, they might. It was a typically beautiful day on the Gulf of Mexico in the western Florida panhandle.

An Old Man was sitting in the shade of his umbrella, reading when he wasn't watching the people around him. Though the book was good and interesting, the people must have been more interesting.

His attention was captured by a family; father, mother and son, coming onto the beach and settling their chairs into the sand. They didn't have an umbrella. The boy had a long, thin, box with bright colors printed on the sides. The Old Man determined that the box contained a kite.

And it did.

After the family was settled in, the boy opened the box and pulled out the kite. He and his father poured over the instruction sheet. The Old Man turned back to his book. He read a couple of pages and glanced up at the man and boy struggling with the instructions. The Old Man smiled as he recalled the hundreds of kites he had built and flown in his lifetime. He had even designed his own kites. He remembered one that was close to six feet across. It looked heavy but it flew, high.

Stories My Mother Never Told Me

The father turned plastic struts over to various angles, trying to match them to the instruction sheet diagrams. He lifted the diamond shaped plastic sails. From experience the Old Man knew that these sails would actually take triangular forms as they were folded around the struts. He smiled thinking that the father hadn't realized this yet. But he would.

The Old Man continued to read, glancing at the construction team as they struggled with the kite. But they were making progress. Something must have finally clicked because the father began to fit all the sails and struts together and suddenly, they had a kite!

The boy tied the long yellow ribbons to the two rear corners of the kite, forming its tail. The kite itself was triangular in shape with the six diamond shaped sails becoming twelve triangular sails as they folded over the struts. It was about three feet across. Next the man tied the kite line to the tip of the triangle and then they walked back toward the dunes, away from people, with plenty of room to fly.

The father gave his son the reel of string while he wound out enough line and carried the kite to a

Stories My Mother Never Told Me

point about fifty feet away. He raised the kite as high as he could reach while the ribboned tail fluttered in the breeze and pushed the kite into the air. It rose only a foot or two while the boy yanked on the string, popping the kite upward another couple of feet before dropping back down. In seconds it fluttered back to the sand.

Meanwhile the breeze gusted and faded. The Old Man knew that if they could get the kite to an altitude that was higher than the tops of the dunes, the kite would rise into the sky. But they struggled, over and over, with little luck. Their frustration was beginning to show, even from this distance.

The Old Man also knew what the problems were. First the yellow ribbons had to go. They were too long and were actually dragging the kite back to the ground. And the kite would never fly with the line attached to the point. It prevented the kite from achieving its natural balance.

He watched for five minutes and could see the frustration of the man and boy continue to rise. Finally, the Old Man knew that he had to act. He rose and slowly walked through the clinging loose sand. He approached the man and boy.

Stories My Mother Never Told Me

"You don't know me from Adam, I know. And you don't have to listen, but I believe I can help you get your kite into the air. You see, I've been flying kites on these beaches all my life and I know something about the ways of kites, all kinds.

"If you'll let me, I can give you a little advice"

The father looked at the Old Man, at his son and then the kite. After a moment, he shrugged his shoulders and said, "Sure, why not, we can't make it fly, so it won't hurt."

The Old Man smiled and said, "First thing you want to do is loose the tail. Those ribbons may look nice fluttering in the wind but in this light breeze all they do is add drag to the kite and weight it down. In a heavier wind you can put them back on. The boy untied the ribbons.

"The next thing you have to do it untie the line from the tip of the kite. Let me show you how to balance the kite."

He took the kite in hand and untied the line. Then he measured out a length of line that was half again as long as the kite itself from tip to base. He cut it with his pocket knife and tied one end to the

Stories My Mother Never Told Me

tip of the kite and the other end to the base. He hung the kite from the string over his finger and let it hang.

"A kite wants to be balanced. If it is, it will want to fly and it will tell you how it wants to be rigged. So, we make a yoke." He turned the kite into the breeze and hooked his finger over the line and let it slide. The line moved to a point about three quarters of the way up between the base and the tip.

"See that? That's the balance point of the kite. That's where you need to rig it. But there's a trick to it." He took the free end of the rest of the kite line and tied it around the point in the yoke where it had balanced on his finger.

"See? This is the balance point. If you tie the line too loose it will move too freely up and down the yoke and will keep the kite from balancing. If you tie it too tight it won't move and if the kite wants to change its balance point, it won't be able to. Here, slide the knot up and down the yoke."

"But if I do that, won't you lose the balance point?" The man asked.

Stories My Mother Never Told Me

"No, I remember where it is. Slide the knot so you can see how tight it should be. Initially it may be necessary to slide it a little either way, but you'll get the balance point just right. I think it's close enough now.

"Something else. Once you have it up a few feet, whatever you do, do not give it much line. Make it ask for line and you'll know when it wants it." He looked at the boy as he spoke. "The other thing is not to give it line too fast. Like I said, make the kite ask for line. If you give it to much it will stall, no matter how strong the wind and it will crash. Keep the line taut and you'll be fine. But pay attention to the kite. It'll tell you what you have to do. Are you ready to give her a try?"

The boy nodded as he backed away with the spool of line and the father held the kite into the breeze. The Old Man told the man to make the line tauter, so the father backed a few feet farther down the beach.

"Don't let any line out until it's at least ten to fifteen feet high. Make it ask!" He called to the boy.

The boy nodded.

Stories My Mother Never Told Me

At that moment the breeze strengthened and the father tossed the kite into the air. It immediately climbed, ten, fifteen, twenty feet and then it was higher than the dunes.

"Give her a little now, you can feel it tugging, its asking, so let it fly!"

The boy carefully metered line and the kite took it gladly and swiftly rose, catching the wind and climbing higher and higher.

"If you anchor the line to the ground, the kite will stay there all day, you bet."

With that the Old Man walked back to his chair. He folded it and put it into its bag. He folded the umbrella, picked up his book and slogged through the sand to his car. He climbed into the driver's seat and started the motor. He craned his neck a bit to look up through the windshield and he could see the kite. Flying high with the light clouds as a backdrop.

"It's not as much fun as flying it myself, but I feel good." He turned the car and drove away.

Stories My Mother Never Told Me

Stories My Mother Never Told Me

The Ants

An email friend and I chatted a lot on line. I told her about the Fire Ant mounds that I had seen in a field on one of my walks. Fire ants are common here in Alabama. She was afraid of them because of their bite. Sometimes that's all it takes to come up with the plot of a story.

It seemed like just another normal day. The temperature was just about perfect and the sky was as clear as his mother's eyes. It was a perfect day for a long walk. So, he said, "to hell with work" and stepped out his front door.

Little did he know he would never step back through it.

The drive to his favorite walking trail was brief and when he got there, he grabbed his walking stick and set off, through the woods, past the swamp and into the fields. He liked it there in the fields because the area was wide open and the sun shone warm and strong on his body. And today was the perfect day.

Stories My Mother Never Told Me

The path through the woods and by the swamp was beautiful today. He could hear squirrels prancing though the undercover and the birds sang cheerfully as he walked. The path swept beside the swamp, which was in the woods, for quite a while. He enjoyed this area. The turtles lined themselves up on outstretched logs to bathe in the dappled sunlight. As he passed most of them splashed into the water in alarm.

Suddenly he heard a commotion nearby. He turned and saw two turkeys scrambling away from the swamp and deeper into the woods until they disappeared from view. Occasionally he saw deer that came to drink but not today.

Soon he came to the edge of the woods and sauntered out into the open field. As he walked the sun did feel warm and the breeze was fragrant with the aroma of Honeysuckle. It almost made him dizzy as he breathed deeply.

He walked on and soon came to a pile of fine earth that was about three feet high. He hadn't seen one this high before. It looked like it was composed of brownish red grains of sand but he knew that it was tiny red clay pellets.

Stories My Mother Never Told Me

Devilishly he prodded the hill to see what would happen. Almost immediately the hill was covered with swarms, millions, of **killer ants**! And they headed straight for him. Mesmerized he watched them as they advanced. In seconds they covered his shoes and then his white socks. Before he knew it his legs were a mass of squirming, ravenous, dark colored ants.

Then they began biting.

They bit his legs as more clambered over the existing ant pants he was now wearing and up his torso. Meanwhile others crawled inside the legs of his shorts and began to bite in places that were very sensitive. It was very unpleasant.

Madly, and in pain, he brushed at the swarming ants but to no avail. It seemed that the more he brushed the more and faster they came. Soon they covered his chest and worked themselves inside his tee shirt and began to do havoc there. He swung his walking stick as though it would accomplish something but all it did was make him look like a mad conductor timing the beat of the army attacking him.

Stories My Mother Never Told Me

Soon they got into his mouth and nose. Then they attacked his eyes and ears. Any opening was soon filled with the vengeful ants. He cried and it was his last cry. His airway was filled with ants and they kept on coming. He fell to the ground writhing as they covered him in a dark wriggling blanket so thick that it was hard to determine whether it was a human or something else lying on the earth.

Finally, he lay still.

Two days later most of him was feeding the millions of ants in the colony and all that could be seen were his bones and clothing.

The ants go in, the ants go out...

Stories My Mother Never Told Me

Hell

In the ancient of days, I was a minister in Pennsylvania. The story of Hell came to me after a minister friend of mine and I had a discussion on the final Christian victory. Of course, I don't believe in Hell, or heaven for that matter, but I think it makes a dandy story.

It was colder than Hell, so to speak. He sat there and shivered in the freezing dark emptiness that was his home. It surely wasn't like the good old days. Back when the furnaces were going full blast and everything was toasty and warm. No, it wasn't like that at all. Now it was just damn freezing cold. He hitched his shoulders and slashed his tail in frustration. He grasped his pitchfork and groaned.

No, it wasn't like the good old days. Why back in the day they were lining up to get into the place. That was the hell of it. The place was getting so packed that he had to expand in to the farther reaches just to accommodate all the new recruits.

What with the wars, especially the Israeli and Iranian nuclear conflict, the sectarian violence and

Stories My Mother Never Told Me

the pure macho killing instinct of those who had nothing; Hell was bursting at the seams. Oh how he loved those days.

His favorite recruits were those who killed each other because of their 'faith" in Allah, or God, or Shamu for all he cared. It didn't matter what, or who, they believed in. It only mattered that they killed each other in great numbers.

At first, when they started streaming in, he treated them like all the rest. He sent them to the fiery pits to shovel endless mountains of coal into the maws of furnaces large enough to swallow entire stadiums. He had thousands of those furnaces and they all needed stoking. But then one day, as he was making his rounds, he heard one complain that this wasn't the paradise he had expected. He also heard something about virgins. That's where he got the idea.

With a team of his best special effects daemons, he created Paradise. Then he set a special watch for those who expected the joys of this paradise and they were ushered right in. Oh, it was grand. The raw recruits were welcomed with open arms. They were given clean robes, figs, wine and all

Stories My Mother Never Told Me

the rest. They were made to feel like kings, or at least princes. And oh, how they loved it. Sucking it all up. Bragging to their fellows about how many they had killed when they became martyrs.

Martyrs, he scoffed to himself. Fools was more like it! They actually believed that pap from their prophet. Didn't they know there was only one prophet and *he* wasn't *their* prophet? But the best part was yet to come.

They kept asking about the virgins. His cohorts kept promising them; the virgins. They would arrive any day. The stories they were told, when alive, filled their heads to bursting with all the sexual fantasies they could imagine. Oh, how he laughed when he thought of them.

Finally, the day came when the seventy-two virgins were introduced. Each stooge was taken to his own room to prepare. How they preened and danced and drank. They might not have had alcohol on earth but they sure took their fill down here.

He went, himself, to the first encounter. He acted the part of a servant. "Master, are you ready? The virgins are just outside that door. Are you ready?"

Stories My Mother Never Told Me

The stooge certainly was. He was drooling as he watched the door slowly open and the first female figure enter. Soon the room was filled with swirling silks as the virgins paraded around the drunken lout. Finally, the dupe lay back on his divan and gestured to one of the virgins. She came to him and he told her to disrobe and to give him service. Slowly, provocatively, she removed her robes to stand before the drunk. There in all her glory stood the old hag. Her dugs hanging to her belly along with the rest of her wrinkles. She smiled a toothless smile and cackled as the stooge gasped in horror.

It was *great*. All the rest of the hags did the same, much to the drunk's fear and amazement. Eventually. he gasped, "Where are all the virgins?"

"You're looking at them!" He replied.

"But they're not young and beautiful. They're old and ugly. I didn't kill myself for that!"

"Oh yes you did! No one promised you young, nubile and beautiful virgins. Just virgins. Be happy that they're female and human. I could have brought you pigs, you know," He grinned. "Oh and by the way, the party's over. You got your wine, virgins and song. You refused the virgins, so that's it for you."

Stories My Mother Never Told Me

He waved his hand and the surroundings were turned into desert sand.

"I might as well be in Hell!" the stooge cried.

"Where do you think you are?" He replied as he sent him off to stoke the furnaces. Oh, how he loved that joke. They were almost as much fun as the lobbyists. He let them sit around for months on end as they dickered for better positions in the hierarchy of Hell. Oh, they knew where they were, all right, they just wanted a better deal. Mix them with politicians and it was one hell of a show.

But then one day something he couldn't explain happened. They didn't come streaming in as fast as usual, finally the immigration slowed to a trickle and then dried up all together. He was so concerned that he actually took a trip topside to see what had happened.

He was stunned. The planet was a barren wasteland. The earth was scorched and dry. It looked and felt a lot like his own home. There wasn't a person to be found. The last human had died and that was that. He wept that day, for the humanity, or lack of it. No more recruits. But Hell was still a bustling and hot property.

Stories My Mother Never Told Me

But then the second thing began to happen.

Thousands of years ago he had made a bet that it would never take place. But now it looked like he was losing it. The bet? It was a simple one he had made with his counterpart. His counterpart, call him God for lack of a better term, had made a third bet with him. The first two were over a man named Job and he had lost miserably over both of them. The worst part was that he thought he was winning; right up to the very end.

So, to get his self-respect back he made a third bet, and it was a sure winner, or so he thought. It was quite simple, not much to it at all. His counterpart had simply said, "You know of my prophet Jesus, don't you? Well, he is my son and he *is* Lord."

He replied "So you say."

"I do say, and to prove it I'll make a bet with you. After all I'm sure you want to recoup your losses from the last two, don't you."

"You know I do. What are the terms?"

Stories My Mother Never Told Me

"Oh, they're really very simple. I'll bet you that you, yourself, will say that Jesus is Lord. And on that day my victory will be complete."

"Ha! And if I don't."

"I'll shut the place down and you can have it all."

He thought that his counterpart had surely made the most foolish bet of all time, and all time was a very long time indeed. "You're on! Hell will freeze over before I do that," he said.

And the bet *was* on.

At first it was so slow that he didn't notice. But as the temperature gradually began to drop a degree here and a degree there, he knew that something was indeed happening. His investigations showed that there were some borderline cases, individuals who could have gone either way but slipped his way due to some slight cause or another, were denying his power and claiming this Jesus' Lordship. And when they did, they were gone.

The problem was that the word spread. As more and more heard of this miraculous way to

Stories My Mother Never Told Me

escape the fiery pits they too did the same. And with a pop, as air filled the vacuum, they were gone, their shovels dropping to clatter on the piles of coal; no longer to stoke the furnaces of Hell.

It really began to hurt when the stooges, the martyrs, began to get the idea and with it the belief. For just saying it didn't work, as many found out. They actually had to believe what they said. When the stooges began to believe, he became just a wee bit worried.

But he shrugged it off. There was no way that his diehards would ever leave the fold. They were faithful only to him. Then one day Shagrat, one of his favorites, was gone and soon the others followed. The furnaces began to go out, for the work force was decimated.

And it began to get cold, colder than hell. Then came the ice; until the very center of hell was an enormous rink, mirror smooth. So smooth that he could see his ugly reflection when he looked down. The final straw was when that old bitch of a wife came to him and said, "Give it up, old man. Can't you see you've lost? We're the only two left in the entire place and I'm leaving."

Stories My Mother Never Told Me

"You're leaving? You're leaving?" he cried.

"Damn right I am! I can't stand the cold. I've had enough." And with that she was gone.

So, he sat there, alone, and shivered in the freezing, dark emptiness that was his empire. It surely wasn't like the good old days. Back when the furnaces were going full blast and everything was toasty and warm. No, it wasn't like that at all. Now it was just damn freezing cold. He hitched his shoulders and slashed his tail in frustration. He grasped his pitchfork and groaned.

"Oh, the hell with it!" He said, "Jesus *is* Lord"

And he was gone.

Stories My Mother Never Told Me

https://www.spacesatmap.us.com[1]

This little tale came to me as I was reading a huge volume of H.P. Lovecraft. So, this is a modern Lovecraftian story. Meet Sam, the millionaire, he has almost everything...

Dr. Sam Browning, in his own mind, was a success. He was nearing his first million and had decided that his bright future included a new home. That he *was* successful there could be no doubt. Graduating in 1995 at twenty-two with a degree in computer science he was already a wiz at the various operating systems such as UNIX and Windows. He was especially proficient with the new Windows 95 operating system. Computers and software

---

[1] At the time of this writing this web site did not exist. Apologies if it does now.

Stories My Mother Never Told Me

development was not only what he would make his carrier but was his hobby as well.

Not long after he earned his degree, he won a job with the Army and began working on Redstone Arsenal in his home town, Huntsville, Alabama. At the same time, he entered graduate school in order to earn his master's degree and later his doctorate.

Sam's job evaluations were excellent from the start. The program he was working for was changing from a UNIX based operating system that used obscure databases to Windows 95. Sam was one of the few in his office that knew anything at all about this new Windows OS. And Sam knew the most; he was, after all, the expert.

As such he was soon assigned the task of converting the complete document management system from UNIX to Windows with an Oracle database. And so he set to work, not for the first time becoming an expert in the workings of the existing system but also the expert leading the conversion of it. He interviewed everyone on site who had anything to do with using the old system and learned what they liked and disliked about it. And then he began to code. After eighteen months, he

Stories My Mother Never Told Me

single-handedly built a completely new system that replaced and improved on the old. He immediately received a promotion and a raise. Starting at a GS7 level he rose to GS9 with that accomplishment and for the rest of his carrier he would continue to rise through the ranks until he hit the top. Along the way he became, at least for a time, an expert in aircraft readiness, missile recap, data transmission and in the end big data analysis,

He retired from the government in 2018 at the ripe old age of 46.

Sam never married and never took on the trappings of his position or income. In fact, while he worked, starting from the first day, he invested the maximum of his income into his government retirement account. He also privately invested as much as he could as well. He lived modestly in a small home, which of course, was paid for. He *did* surround himself with computers and other related equipment. When he got home from work, he immediately sat down at his development computer and continued working on his personal or freelanced projects.

Stories My Mother Never Told Me

Because he was a freelance software developer, he made some very good money working on the side, providing his freelance work to local DoD contractors and to anyone who had the cash to pay for his work. All in all he made a tidy bundle.

And then around 2015 he got interested in day trading and so continued to build his wealth to the point where he had complete independence. He owed nobody anything and that's how he liked it. A good friend taught him the ins and outs and so he continued to get richer.

Nowadays he spent his morning hours working what he called his trading desk. In the afternoons and evenings, he would write software, play games (he was a big gamer) and just pretty much noodle around. He also had been thinking about looking for a new house where he could have a bit more privacy and a larger living environment and computer room.

It was then that he discovered the web site https://spacesatmap.us.com. It put Google maps to shame as well as any other satellite mapping web site. Spacesatmap, among other brilliant concepts kept an online catalogue of all its photos. That

Stories My Mother Never Told Me

meant that a person could look at a satellite photo that was taken a few months ago and then page back through all of the existing photos that had been taken in the past of the same general location. Thus, the growth in an area could be historically tracked; new developments could be followed through to their completion.

One photo that Sam particularly liked was what he called the lawn ornament shot. It was even in his own neighborhood. He lived in the landing path of the airport and so had many airplanes flying overhead – one of the reasons he was thinking of moving. This one satellite photo had captured an airplane in the landing pattern when it was exactly over a nearby vacant corner lot. Because of the low altitude of the airplane and the high altitude of the satellite the airplane was perfectly in focus with the earth. It looked like the plane was sitting on the ground. Sam though it was a hilarious photo. In fact for a while, he had it as the wallpaper on his main monitor.

The other thing that he liked about this web site was the detail and clarity of the photographs. Sites like Google might show people as little dots on the screen with no more detail but Spacesatmap

Stories My Mother Never Told Me

actually had enough detail to show whether a person was wearing a hat and you could even discern the brighter colors. He would not have been surprised if he could have read licence plate numbers but the angle was usually wrong. And the detail was in every photograph, not just the well populated areas but the countryside in the middle of nowhere itself. Sam found himself exploring more and more of the world with this fantastic tool.

Of course, he used it to start looking for a new place to live. He wanted to find a place to build or buy that had a bit of privacy, not that he had anything to hide, but because he liked being alone. That was one reason he never considered marriage or even had a steady girlfriend. He was happy the way things were. He could do what he wanted, when he wanted and had nobody to answer to. That was the way life was supposed to be lived and that's the way he lived it.

Sometimes he found things in the satellite photos that amused or surprised him. Once he found a photo that had an obviously naked couple having sex on the flat roof, or deck, of a house. He had seen a couple of automobile accidents as well. He assumed that if a person looked, scenes like these

Stories My Mother Never Told Me

would be more common than one might would expect.

And then he found the house. It was across town, to the north-west, sitting on what looked like a one-acre plot. It was gated and looked like it had a fence surrounding the property. The house itself looked to be a brick home, solid and long lasting. There was a single car in the driveway. Sam found it curious that the color of this house and property looked off, as though the photo had faded. In fact, the color looked like it came from a fifty-year-old print while the surrounding area was in bright colors. He knew that satellite photos were not always uniform, that sunlight, time of day, weather conditions and more could affect the color of a photograph but usually that was noticeable when different photos were butted together that were taken at different times.

He looked back through the history of the shot and found the same color anomaly in every photo in the past. Not only that, but the car never moved. Now *that* was curious, something that he would have to take a look at personally. After all, he had the time.

Stories My Mother Never Told Me

Next, he switched to Google's Street view and quickly found the address. When the little man dropped onto the spot on the map, Sam spun him around to face the property. He could clearly see the gated wall facing the street but could not see much through the gate itself. It appeared to be covered with vines. He did note that the color in the street view was bright and natural.

A few days later he grabbed his camera and decided to investigate. He took the parkway and then 565 to the RPB and on to where the house was located. It was a nice sunny July day. The temperatures were in the high 80s, typical for this time of year. As he neared the house, he noticed that there were no houses close by. He wondered why he hadn't noticed that in the satellite photos.

He pulled up to the gate and climbed from his car. The heat hit him immediately as he left the air-conditioned SUV and he began to sweat. He took his camera and walked around his car the short distance to the gate. Of course, it was bolted and locked. He peered through the vines and could see the house a couple of hundred yards away. The driveway curved away from the gate to run around the right periphery of the property and then turn to

Stories My Mother Never Told Me

what Sam assumed would be the garage. That, he also assumed, would be where the car was parked.

The place looked abandoned.

Poking the camera lens through the vines he took a couple of photos of the house with his telephoto lens. Pulling some of the vines away from the gate Sam got a better look at the house, it looked like a very nice house, two stories, a tall columned entrance with a tall front door and windows and shrubbery surrounding the home. The lawn was a bit dry and browning as though it had not been watered for a while but it was not tall and there were no visible weeds.

From his vantage point the roof looked like it was in good shape. But the place looked deserted, like there had been nobody on the property for quite a while. Sam could certainly not fathom this. Why would a house worth a good half million – or more, be empty. It didn't make sense.

It was getting late and traffic would soon be growing as everyone left the arsenal at the end of the work day so Sam decided to return home. At least he had some photos of the place but he was more intrigued than ever. The next time he went, he would be prepared to spend some time, so that he could walk the perimeter of the property and maybe even find a way through what he believed to be a surrounding fence. It was something he looked forward to doing.

When he arrived back home, he immediately went to his computer and pulled the SD card from his camera and inserted it into the slot of the computer. He did not expect what he saw.

The photos were all very clear and in sharp focus. The detail was excellent but the color in each and every one was the exact same faded shade that he had seen in the satellite photos. They looked like they had been taken fifty years earlier and had been left out in the sunlight too long. The colors were faded and tended toward the red/orange end of the spectrum. The greens were muted.

The photos he had taken of the surrounding area and the gates were in perfect color it was just that those taken through the gate were really odd. It was something that Sam simply could not fathom. It stuck with him for days.

He decided that the next time he went he would launch his drone and get close aerial video of

Stories My Mother Never Told Me

the place. He'd walk around first in hopes of finding a good place to launch. The drone had an excellent HD camera and he had used it frequently. In fact, he made videos and posted some of his better work online.

In the mornings, though, he continued his daily trading activities and was making some very good investments. He found that often by buying early in the day, when the markets opened and were rising that he could sell a few hours later and rake in a few bucks. It worked well for him and his strategy was paying off.

He still had software projects that he had to work on so his free time was somewhat limited. But he would make time for the house; that was for sure.

His drone was a popular high-end model, commonly called a quadcopter and on the box, itself, was called a "flying video platform." It was easy to fly and returned excellent video and stills, though he rarely took stills. Its legal top altitude was four hundred feet and so he was comfortable flying it fairly high. He was more careful about the distance of how far away the drone was from himself when he flew. If he, or a watcher, could no longer see it, even

Stories My Mother Never Told Me

though he could see *exactly* where the drone was from the video it was transmitting to his tablet, he still got a little nervous. He didn't want to lose this expensive toy. He knew that when he got back to the house, he could get excellent areal video of the place. He could even fly low around the house and get some good close-up work, close to eye level. With a twenty-minute battery life he could get some excellent video. One good sunny day he would take the trip again, that was a given.

Almost a week passed before he was again able to return. It was another beautiful hot Alabama summer's day. The temperature was in the nineties and the humidity was through the roof. He knew that it would be uncomfortable but the air was dead still and he liked it that way.

He pulled up to the gate and locked his car. He didn't even take his camera but he did take the drone. First, he simply wanted to walk around to look for a good launching place or a way through the fence. He wanted to make sure there was really nobody home. He'd cross that fence when he got to it.

Stories My Mother Never Told Me

The area between the wall and the road was mostly gravel and had few weeds and grass growing on it. When he rounded the end of the wall, however, there was a bit more undergrowth but it was not daunting. Sam plowed forward.

There was no path but, to his right, Sam could see a fence, not a single wire, but a chain link fence used to keep animals, and other things, out; the fence rose to about six feet from the ground. Much of it was overgrown with vines, some of it looking like poison ivy. He would definitely steer clear of that.

Undaunted Sam walked on. The heat and humidity was beginning to get to him as were the insects, especially flies that buzzed at his head and gnats that constantly fluttered around him. He was almost constantly waving his hands. 'Too bad I don't smoke,' he thought. Through and over the fence he could see the large lawn with the house firmly planted to the rear. Now Sam could see clearly that there were few weeds in the lawn and though it looked dry and faded, the grass itself was not tall at all. It looked like it hadn't been mowed in about two weeks but Sam was sure that it had been much longer than that.

Stories My Mother Never Told Me

A couple of hundred feet along the fence he found what he had hoped would exist. There, at one spot, the fence looked like it had been pulled down and, when he approached it, he found he could step over it without too much trouble. Rather than do that now, he decided to continue along the fence until he had made a complete circle or was stopped by some unsurmountable obstacle.

And so, he walked on in the heat and bugs. He was almost used to both by now. Ahead he could see that the path, such as it was, ended – or turned a corner – along a wooded area. Hopefully that would be a little cooler. The day was quiet. He didn't hear birds or see animals like squirrels and chipmunks. He definitely saw no animals on or around the house. Within a few minutes he reached the end of the current path and found himself at a corner. He turned right and began to follow the rear line of the property. The trees did overhang the path and it was a bit more comfortable.

It took Sam a few moments to realize that there was no fence to his right. Apparently, it ended at the corner he had just rounded. All he had to do now was to step into the lawn behind the house. And he did so.

Stories My Mother Never Told Me

He was now only about one hundred feet from the rear of the house. He could see a deck along the back side. There was no sign of a garden, trees or even a simple swing. He stood there looking at the house. Nothing moved, there were no movements behind the windows. On the deck he could see a chair lying on its side as though toppled by the wind. He could clearly see a grill, shiny in the shade of the overhanging roof above the deck. It all looked so peaceful and at the same time he had a feeling of expectation – as though something was about to happen; people congregating on the deck, cold beaded cans of beer in their hands, someone at the grill, cooking. But noting moved and the air was still.

Feeling he was taking a great risk, he still felt compelled to try to launch the drone. Sam took a few steps into the back yard, not noticing that the grass made a crunching sound under his feet. He carefully placed the drone and started it. Then he turned on the tablet computer and flight controller. Within seconds the controller was ready to connect to the drone and to the tablet. Sam completed the connections. The tablet now controlled the drone. He swiveled the drone's camera to test the connection. Then he pointed the camera straight down. On the

Stories My Mother Never Told Me

tablet's screen he could see the small patch of grass where the camera was aimed.

When the software indicated that the GPS connection had been made Sam brushed over the launch panel on the screen and the drone's motors started. It lifted straight up to an altitude of about three feet and hung there in the silent summer air – waiting for a command.

Sam pushed the left joystick forward the drone leapt into the air and climbed rapidly to an altitude of one hundred fifty feet. Sam let go of the joystick and the drone hung there, waiting. Sam turned the drone and as he did so he manipulated the camera until he could see the house centered on the tablet's screen.

Then he flew over the house, looking down. He could see the car in the driveway far below. To Sam the roof looked good and solid. After a few minutes he brought the drone to an altitude of about fifteen feet and flew around the house, rotating the drone so that the camera always pointed towards the house. All the while he could see no movement in the house itself as he looked, as best he could, through the windows.

Stories My Mother Never Told Me

As he flew along the deck at the rear of the house, he could see the stainless-steel gas grill and deck furniture. One chair was laying on its side. He could see nothing more. After a couple of minutes, he flew the drone back to himself and landed it. He turned everything off and put the controller and tablet next to the drone, there in the dry grass. Somehow, he knew it would be quite safe right where it was. He was anxious to see the video when he got home.

Now Sam ventured out into the lawn, watching the house closely for any movement, and approached the deck. The closer he got, the surer he was that there was nobody there and that nobody had been there for perhaps - years. Surely the buzz of the drone would have brought someone out if there were anyone home. Soon he found himself at the first step leading up to the deck. He took it.

The deck was solid and clean. The only thing out of place was the chair which he righted and pushed to the glass topped table. Sam turned and leaned on the deck rail and surveyed the back yard. This was the kind of place he was looking for. He wondered if it was for sale and was determined to do the research to find out. But he remembered that

Stories My Mother Never Told Me

there was no For Sale sign at the front gate. If it *was* for sale there should be a sign.

Fully realizing that he was trespassing he decided to be hung for a wolf instead of a sheep. He walked to the French doors leading into the house and peered through the glass panes.

The interior of the house was dimly lit. He could see light streaming through the windows in the front of the house painting stripes of bright light on the floor. But the back part of the house was harder to discern. He could see furniture, a sectional couch, what might be a lounge chair. To the right there appeared to be a bar, possibly it was near the kitchen. He could see little else.

On impulse he tried the door knob. It didn't fully turn but it didn't feel locked either. It felt more like it was stuck, perhaps from disuse. Though he was briefly tempted, Sam did not pull very hard on the door but, instead, continued his explorations.

Leaving the deck, he walked around the house. At the back there were no other doors, save a trap door that led to the crawl space. He definitely was not going in there. As he rounded the corner to the south side of the house, he saw the Cadillac

Stories My Mother Never Told Me

parked in the driveway facing a three-car garage. The garage rollup doors were closed and the side door itself was locked. Sam didn't try to raise the garage doors.

He did look at the car, though. It was about four or five years old. It needed washing, though it was more dusty than dirty. The doors were locked and he could see nothing on the seats. The tires were obviously low on air. Sam knew the car hadn't moved in years. The satellite images told him that. He continued around the house. As he rounded to the front of the house, he encountered the flower beds that hugged the front of the house. They were untended and very little grew in them. Here and there a dandelion. Up against the house itself there were a number of low juniper bushes and at the corners of the entry were stunted holly trees. He had never seen holly's that were stunted in their growth like these two. He stood there, in front of the house and surveyed the property. He liked what he was looking at but at the same time felt a bit of unease. He marked that down to the fact that he was trespassing. But then, he thought, 'there's nobody here at all. The place is empty.'

Stories My Mother Never Told Me

A bit bolder now he took the three steps to the porch and the front door. He was surprised to see that the doorbell was lit. He had assumed that the power had been disconnected. He was tempted to ring the bell but his better nature took hold and he tried the door latch itself. It didn't give.

Sam continued his tour around the house and soon found himself at the deck in the rear. Having learned next to nothing he returned to the path at the rear of the property and resumed his tour around the periphery. Five minutes later he was back at his car. Hot and sweating he wished for a drink. He put the drone equipment into the back of the car and he got into the front and started it. Within a few minutes he could feel the cool air begin to bathe his face. It felt really good.

Sam drove home.

The drone video was sharp, as he expected. Sam wasn't surprised to see that the color of the video was faded. 'But why doesn't it look faded to me when I'm there? It must be something in the lenses or the camera electronics.'

He watched the video again. At the drone's highest altitude, the field of view of the camera

Stories My Mother Never Told Me

extended beyond what Sam assumed was the property line. *And the color of the foliage on the other side was as natural as the trees behind his own house.*

A chill briefly ran down Sam's spine.

He tried to put thoughts of the house out of his mind as he went about his daily business, trading and coding. But it kept intruding. The desire became stronger and stronger. He even began to dream about the house.

In his dream he went up onto the deck and opened the door. The interior of the house was dim and covered in dust. There was a large modern kitchen with all the appliances. He opened the refrigerator and the light came on and the interior, though empty, was cold. The large living room had a gas fireplace, a very large flat screen television and a sectional couch. There were other rooms on the first floor including an office and toilets. On the second floor there were three bedrooms and two baths. All furnished. The third floor consisted of a large open attic. This room was nearly bare.

In his waking time, he plotted on how to enter the house. Though he knew nothing about picking

Stories My Mother Never Told Me

locks, he purchased a lock picking kit from an online seller and received it overnight.

He practiced, following the instructions, until he could fumble open the included padlock. Then he worked on his own front door until he could manage to unlock it. He decided that he was ready. He would get into that house, one way or another.

That night he again dreamed about the house. This time he thought he heard people talking and moving inside the house, but he saw nothing. The following morning, he got his camera and lock pick kit and went to the house. 'Maybe the back door will open if I pull hard enough.' He thought as he drove. He wasn't very confident of being able to unlock the doors, though he would definitely try. He would get inside, one way or another.

He parked in the usual place and walked around the edge of the property, never thinking about trying to pick the front gate's lock. He reached the opening in the fence and stepped through into the back yard. He scanned the property but saw noting and no one. Sam boldly walked through the yard and up onto the deck. There he tried the door again. The knob turned and he pulled. On the third

Stories My Mother Never Told Me

strong tug the door suddenly opened and he almost fell back.

He froze and waited for something to happen. To hear an alarm or a person in the house coming to see what the commotion was. But nothing happened. Finally, he gingerly stepped into the house.

He could clearly see that he was in the living room. It was large and looked comfortable. The ceiling was about ten feet high and bordered with ornate crown moulding. There was a sectional couch, a lounge chair and coffee table. On the wall was a large flatscreen television. There was even a gas fireplace in the corner. It was almost exactly as he had dreamed.

The air was dry and smelled faintly of cinnamon. He turned to his right and looked into the kitchen alcove where a table and four chairs were arranged in the bay window. He carefully stepped into the alcove. There he swung left into the kitchen itself. There was plenty of counterspace, a gas stove and oven along with a large refrigerator. Sam could hear it running. The cabinets were spacious. He opened one and saw that it was filled with China. On the counter there was a coffee maker and mugs hung

Stories My Mother Never Told Me

from the underside of the cabinets. There was a large double tub sink next to the built-in dishwasher. To the right there was a small pantry. There a doorway led to the rest of the house.

He stepped through into a hallway. Directly ahead was the dining room with a large table and six chairs. 'Very nice.' He thought.

Exploring the rest of the first floor he found the office, that he somehow expected, a toilet, and what he assumed was a den with book cases, a writing desk and chairs. On the table was a brandy decanter and four snifters. There was brandy in the decanter. Sam was tempted to pull the stopper to take a sniff. But he had decided to touch nothing. In the corner was a properly outfitted wet bar which was well stocked with liquor and wine. Everything was covered with dust.

Going upstairs he found four bedrooms. All beautifully appointed with large beds. The master bedroom was indeed large and well outfitted with a fireplace, dry bar and large TV. The master bath seemed to be as large as a small apartment. It had a sun roof.

Stories My Mother Never Told Me

In the upstairs hall was a door that obviously led to the attic. He gingerly took the steps, one at a time. As he climbed, he could feel the temperature rise. Until this moment he had not realized that the house, proper, had been comfortably cool, though he had not heard the air conditioning run.

As he stepped into the attic, he saw that the large room was almost completely empty. The room was dimly lit from the dormers built into the high peaked roof. All that was in the room were a couple of chairs and a table. There was something on the table.

Sam stepped across the room. He was drawn to the table and the object on it. The object appeared to shimmer and glow in the dim light. Sam could see that the object looked like it had melted in the heat of the attic. It was oblong and about a foot long on the longest side. It mounded in the center to about four inches. As he looked closer, he could see that it shimmered in the dim light and he could almost hear it hum.

It was rainbow colored and the colors swirled and glowed in constant motion. It was mesmerizing and Sam had to consciously pull his attention away

Stories My Mother Never Told Me

from the object. He felt as though it wanted to pull him in.

Though he knew that he shouldn't, he touched it. The hum immediately filled his body like both a musical tone and a vibration. The object was warm to the touch and he felt suddenly peaceful. He could stay here all day.

Then everything shifted. The room seemed to make a ninety-degree turn. Everything blurred before him and he felt flooded with vertigo. The hum took on a deeper, more intense tone and the vibration began to feel more like an electric shock.

Then everything became dark and he believed he could see the stars, as though he were outside at night. The just as quickly, almost with an audible snap, the world righted itself and he was standing in a hot attic. The object no longer glowed and shimmered. There was no hum or vibration. It was simply something that had melted in the summers heat over many years.

Finding nothing else of interest, Sam left not only the attic but the house itself. As he went through the door onto the deck, he pulled the door sharply closed. It latched shut as the lock clicked.

Stories My Mother Never Told Me

Sam drove home. He felt at ease and somehow satisfied about the house. But he knew that tomorrow he would look into how to purchase the place. He had seen it and he liked it. He knew that he would be comfortable living there.

He didn't notice, as he crossed the lawn, that the grass was slightly greener than it had been when he had arrived. Almost as though it had had a good watering in a summer of drought.

That night he began to have really strange dreams.

In the dreams he was again in the attic of the house. But now the object was not a melted mass but, instead, a fully formed statuette about a foot tall. It was oddly shaped. It had a flat base and barrel shaped body and a head with tentacles atop a short neck. It was greenish in color and felt smooth and slippery, like soapstone. When he picked it up, it vibrated in his hands. He did not want to put it back down and struggled to do so. Then the dream shifted and he was in his own house, standing in his office. He was still holding the statuette. When he finally put it in its new place, on his desk, he still felt

Stories My Mother Never Told Me

the vibrations coursing through his body. He felt more alive than ever.

When he awoke in the morning, though his sleep had been restless and filled with dreams, he felt well rested. In fact, he felt as though he was vibrating, just as he had in the dream. He really did feel more alive than ever.

Interestingly he had also lost interest in the house. He no longer had the desire to visit it. In fact, he had no desire to purchase the property or live there. As the days passed, he lost interest in his day trading and he stopped coding. He didn't even play his video games. He stopped going out.

He never noticed the fact that his lawn seemed to stop growing, or that it began to take on the dry color of the lawn at the house. He didn't notice that the colors of things in his house began to be faded, like an old photograph. Or that his skin began to look transparent. Had he noticed, he could have seen the veins in his hands and even the tendons, as time passed. He didn't notice that he stopped eating or that his hair was falling out.

Stories My Mother Never Told Me

Sam didn't notice anything except the vibration and the hum. The vibration that filled him and made him more alive than ever.

Had Sam looked at the Spacesatmap web site he would have seen that two things had taken place. The house looked as normal as all the surrounding properties, bright and colorful while his own property took on the color of a faded photograph, turning red and orange. But Sam never looked.

Sam noticed noting but the vibration, even as he faded to nothingness there in his faded house. But the strange statuette on his desk began to glow and vibrate and hum, there in the quiet, faded and empty house.

Stories My Mother Never Told Me

John and Marsha

It is said that a successful science fiction story should not use the word vermin, among others, but this one does and I don't give a damn. After all, it's my story. Ogg Vorbis, the character, is modeled after the alien in the Monty Python movie, The Life of Brian, *one of the funniest scenes ever filmed!*

"I wouldn't go out with you if you were the last man on earth!" Marsha shouted at John Riley. She turned and flounced away, her long hair waving in time to her bobbing head.

John sighed and began to shuffle off in the opposite direction. What did she know about anything? Sure, he might be a *little* bit over weight and he did have an acne problem. But he was a decent guy and he had a lot to offer; if only she would take the time to look. He knew, however, that she wouldn't spend the time. No, not Marsha with her valley girl looks and a body to die for. "No, I guess not." John sighed.

Stories My Mother Never Told Me

In truth the only thing that John and Marsha had in common was that they both had fiery red hair.

* * * * *

Ogg Vorbis worked for the Galactic Cleansing Agency. It was one of the top operatives of the GCA. As Ogg's ship cruised through hyperspace it examined the Intergalactic Atlas for the coordinates of the upcoming node. That way it could exit to normal spacetime at the correct point for the next assignment. This prime specimen of Aldorian life was somewhat of a purist when it came to galactic travel. Ogg Vorbis prided itself in its pinpoint accuracy. Ogg also took pride in a job well, if not quickly, done.

"There!" O.V., as it was called for short, had located, with the expected pinpoint accuracy, the exit node. With its eyestalks waving in anticipation, it programmed the biomass computer with the proper coordinates and then took a look at the details of the next cleansing.

Stories My Mother Never Told Me

It appeared to be a water world that was in line for new development in the next couple of thousand years or so, and all the vermin had to be cleansed from the surface of the planet so to make a nice clean slate for the developers to work.

"Piece of shit!" Vorbis exclaimed. Now on Ogg's home planet shit was a fine delicacy that grew in the wild and was harvested by semi-sentient beings specially bred to smell and dig this treat which grew at the base of the tall fernlike rung-rung trees of the hot regions of the planet.

At that moment Ogg's ship popped into normal spacetime and, to its tremendous satisfaction, only a couple of light hours from the target. Now to make quick work of this assignment and then off to a bit of relaxation on the gambling planet Billogcie.

Vorbis steered its ship to the planet in question and then loaded the ship's tanks with the cleansing solution which was called VarmAway. In the ship's red cinnamon light, the color of the solution was a sludge brown. Ogg didn't care what color it was. All it cared about was that it worked like a charm.

Stories My Mother Never Told Me

The ship entered the atmosphere and Ogg opened the vents. After a few passes around the planet the tanks were empty. With a satisfied nod of its eyestalks, it sped back out into space, and on to the gambling planet.

* * * * *

John Riley woke with a pounding headache. He had been out late the night before and had barely made it home. He tried to sit up but immediately hit his head on the underside of his bed. "Ow!" he cried as he crawled out from under it. As he did so he vaguely remembered crawling *under* the bed to get something the night before. For the life of him he couldn't remember what he had been looking for.

He stumbled to the bathroom and scrabbled through the medicine cabinet looking for the ibuprofen. He took four tablets and made his way, half crawling, to the kitchen. Maybe a bite to eat would help soothe his hangover. Funny, though, he didn't remember having anything to drink. He had played video games all night until he was ready to

Stories My Mother Never Told Me

drop but he didn't remember drinking much at all. He sat at the kitchen table, groaned, held his head in his hands and immediately passed out.

Three blocks away Marsha Truman woke with a pounding headache. As *she* tried to sit up, *she* banged *her* head. She winced, opened her eyes and looked directly at the slats that held her box spring in place. "What in hell am I doing under my bed?" she asked herself. Normally she slept on her bed, not *under* it. Duh! She shook her red hair in bemusement, and not a little pain, as she crawled out from under her bed and into the sunlight streaming across the Burberry carpet of her room.

Marsha too indulged in ibuprofen that morning but unlike John, she took a designer brand. Nothing generic for her. She nursed an orange juice and tried to call her friend Sally. When Sally didn't answer her cell phone Marsha sighed and dialed Doris, her next best friend.

Doris didn't answer either. "Where is everybody?" she wondered as she went to the bathroom to take her morning shower. Half an hour later, feeling somewhat refreshed, she stepped out of the shower and grabbed a towel. Her wet hair hung

Stories My Mother Never Told Me

in hanks as she hand dried it in the fluffy towel before blow drying it into perfection. An hour later, after much primping and preening she felt ready to face the world. Her headache was all but forgotten.

Again, she tried calling Sally, then Doris and finally, in pure desperation to talk to *somebody* this morning, she tried calling Annie. When Annie didn't answer, Marsha became depressed, as all of her best friends were obviously ignoring her. Well, a little shopping would cure her blues.

She thought it a little strange that there was no traffic, but all the better for her! She didn't really get upset until she got to the mall and found all the doors locked. She never noticed that the parking lot was almost totally empty, only that she got a choice parking spot.

In the meantime, John woke for the second time of the day. He felt quite a bit better as he rose from the kitchen table. He *was* stiff and thought that a good hot shower would be just the thing.

Later, refreshed from his shower, he decided to take a drive to the mall to see if the video game he had ordered had come in. His street never had much

Stories My Mother Never Told Me

traffic so he didn't notice the lack of it until he hit the main drag.

The parkway was deserted. But what was really odd was the number of wrecks he saw, some of them blocking parts of the highway. "What is going on here?" he wondered as he slowly drove. "Somehow, I don't think the mall is going to be open. Somehow, I think something major has happened here." He turned on the radio but all he got was static.

The mall was no better. When he arrived and saw only a small handful of cars as he drove the circuit, he knew that something *was* wrong. How wrong he didn't know. He also didn't know that he was the last guardian of manhood on a planet - where only one female lived. And it was at that moment that he saw the female.

John slowly pulled his car up to Marsha as she stood dejectedly at the locked door of the Gap entrance. He opened the window and said, "Hi!" as brightly as he could.

"Humph!" Marsha said as she shook her lovely red hair.

Stories My Mother Never Told Me

"There anything that I can do for you?" John hopefully asked.

"Not on your life," Marsha answered.

"Notice anything funny this morning?" John asked.

"Like what? You talking to me?"

"Where is everybody? Haven't you noticed that there's nobody around?"

"People are just running late, that's all. Why they'll open the mall any minute."

"I don't *think* so," John replied. "If you don't mind, I think I'll park over there. I'll stay there for a few hours, just in case"

"What do I care?" Marsha sniffed.

Six hours later Marsha began to care. Nobody answered their phones, the stores remained closed and she began to get hungry. Sullenly she drove back to the mall. John was still parked in the same spot. She pulled up next to him, wound down her window and said, "I'm hungry."

Stories My Mother Never Told Me

John brightly smiled and said; "Let's go to my place. I think I can fix you something good to eat. Do you want to get in, or do you want to follow me?"

"Will I be safe in your kitchen?" Marsha asked. John told her that yes, she would be safe. So, of course, Marsha followed John to his home. Thankfully he kept it neat in his parent's absence. Because his parents were away a lot, he had learned to cook for himself and was pretty good at it. He made pasta.

As they ate Marsha complained about the lack of phone service, the sudden disappearance of her parents and friends, the closed malls and more. John simply listened.

"It's like we're the last two people on earth," Marsha sighed. John grinned.

Neither knew it at the moment but Marsha was right. Ogg Vorbis had almost done its job perfectly. For some reason the cleansing solution didn't work on vermin sleeping under their beds. This was a known situation and the containers clearly stated this fact on the labels. And on the planet it had just cleansed only two of the vermin, in close proximity to each other, had been sleeping

Stories My Mother Never Told Me

under beds. It was the proximity thing that was the problem.

Though Marsha was not immediately happy with the situation, as John lost weight over the next six months, his acne cleared on a new diet and as hormones began to work over time, she finally took a close look at him and said, "Oh what the hell."

* * * * *

Ten thousand years later Ogg Vorbis was fired when the developers arrived to find the planet overrun with red headed vermin.

Stories My Mother Never Told Me

The Dragon in the Woods

My wife and I were sitting on the deck drinking Bombay Saphire martinis. It was a warm June afternoon, a perfect Alabama day. As we sipped, I did look up and I did see a dragon and I did take a photograph of it. And this story wrote itself.

I didn't know there was a dragon in the woods behind the house. I had no idea, until the day I was sitting on the deck with my wife, having a martini. No, I wasn't drunk or hallucinating. It was an early evening in the first week of June.

I took a sip of my gin and looked up – and there he was. At least I think it was a male but how could I tell. "My God!" I nearly shouted to my wife, "There's a dragon in the woods. It looks like it's about to take off. I've got to get the camera!"

To say the least, I was excited. I rushed into the house and into the bedroom where I kept the camera. Hurrying back to the deck I removed the lens cap and turned on the power. Thankfully I already had the telephoto, so I was able to get a good shot of the beast. There he was, nodding his head

Stories My Mother Never Told Me

and rustling his wings, as though he was about to take flight. I watched him for many minutes but he never did leave the ground. Instead, he pranced, nodded his head and flapped his wings. I imagined I could hear him in the woods but he was far enough away that all I could really hear was the wind.

As the days passed, I watched the dragon in the woods. Some days he would prance and dance there among the pines, maple and walnut trees. Other days he would stand silent sentinel, gazing over his domain, watching the children in the neighboring yards innocently playing in his shadow. It amazed me that the children, *children of all people*, never saw him. I guess they never heard him either.

Every day he was there and every day I watched him. Even on rainy days, he would not hide from the rain, deeper in the woods, but instead stood proudly at the edge of the woods, dripping water into the brush at his feet, as he gazed out into the surrounding neighborhood.

I never saw him breathe fire.

More than once in the summer, especially on those days then the cumulous clouds rushed buy the

113

Stories My Mother Never Told Me

sun, alternately throwing him into shadow and sunlight, I swear I saw him smile. On those days when the songbirds were not even afraid of him but instead soared and dove around his head, he would flap his wings in sheer joy of being alive.

I remember one hot night in July when the thunder rolled and the wind whipped around the eaves of the house, moaning and sighing in the corners of the fence and generally being miserable. The lightning flashed in the gusting wind. I went out onto the deck to watch the weather; I like thunder storms. As the lightning flashed, I could see the dragon dancing and jumping in the ghostly white strobe of the storm. I imagined that this time, for the first real time, I could hear him roar back at the groaning clouds and the thrashing rain and hail. He never retreated to his den, not even from the hail. No, he resolutely stood his ground. And it was on that night that I began to understand the dragon and why he was there.

You know, I never saw him leave the woods, not even to chase the hawks away from the squirrels. Instead, he always stood sentinel, gazing through and over the tree tops, standing tall; both stern and benign at the same time. Yes, I knew why he was

Stories My Mother Never Told Me

there and it wasn't, Smaug like, to protect gold or jewels from marauders. In fact, I'm not sure he even had a cave or a shelter of any kind for that matter. I'm sure he had no gold or riches hidden away. He never retreated from his highpoint in the woods. Day or night, storm or sun, he was always there.

He was protecting his domain and all who lived in it.

As the summer passed, his green coat gathered a dusty sheen. I suppose that without rain in August, September or October, and the fact that there is no nearby pond large enough for him to bathe, that the dust of the earth settled onto his green skin. He was bright in the spring, but as late summer and fall approached, he became a bit duller and as November approached, he became mottled and began to look a little tired.

But he never strayed from his duty and once in a while I even think that he knew *I knew* he was watching me personally. One time I was sure I saw him wink. This was obviously no dumb dragon or mean beast. I almost felt as though he and I had become secret friends. I'm sure he knew that I was the only one who was aware of his existence. My wife

115

Stories My Mother Never Told Me

forgot about him even though he watched over her as she worked in her garden every afternoon. He was there, protecting her but she never cared. And the children played near him but never noticed.

Maybe that's the problem. Nobody knew or cared save for me. I, on the other hand, checked on him every day, and I still do. But now, in the depths of winter he is a skeleton of his former self. He looks old, tired and even in a bit of pain. It grieves me to see him like that and I wonder if he will be back to his old self when the spring comes. I certainly hope so because it is hard to watch a friend age and wither before your eyes. The days are short and I think it might be the darkness that has made him so. He always was a creature of the sunlight; unlike other dragons I have known.

Never the less, he still stands sentinel over the neighborhood. Some days shaking his head and shivering his wings, as though ready to take flight. I don't sit on the deck in this weather, it is too cold for me and martinis just aren't the same on a deck in the winter. But whenever I go out to the back yard or onto the deck, I do give the dragon in the woods a wave. I hope to see him well and happy in the spring. I think, for both of us, that time can't come too soon.

Stories My Mother Never Told Me

Here is a photo of the dragon that I took that first June day.

Stories My Mother Never Told Me

King Boots, Spaceport Mouser

Story ideas come to me at the strangest times. This one came to me in the middle of the night and I partially dreamed it – I think.

Since the beginning of time, or at least the beginning of sea trade, rats, mice and other pests have become stowaways. These animals managed to get aboard boats and ships no matter how careful and observant the crews were. It was unavoidable. That's how certain species migrated across the globe, hitching a free ride on a ship.

Even, in later years, discs were placed on ship's mooring ropes, called rat guards, to prevent rats from climbing those ropes and gaining access to the ship. It worked fairly well but rats and other creatures still found their ways onboard through other means.

And it didn't stop with seagoing vessels. Airplanes, trucks, trains and other modes of transportation were also plagued by these stowaways. And as humanity spread out from the Earth into space, distant planets and on to the stars,

Stories My Mother Never Told Me

rats and other vermin found their way aboard no matter how vigilant the ship's crews were.

As a result, rats and mice are everywhere that humanity has travelled and settled. Even here at Spaceport Thevenin.

In its thousand-year existence the history of Spaceport Thevenin has gone from a humble rest stop in the greater cloud to become a major crossroads to the stars and even beyond. It may be mere chance that Thevenin is literally only three weeks from the nearest Chalmers Jump Point, but it took hard work, imagination and ingenuity and a little bit of luck to create the super spaceport of today.

Thevenin is indeed called the crossroads of the stars for the very reason I just mentioned. In no other place in the known universe are there more than three Chalmers Jump points in close proximity and Thevenin has five! That means that Spaceport Thevenin is the busiest spaceport anywhere. On any given day more than fifty ships will arrive or depart. The average number of ships in the docks is well over a hundred on any given day.

Stories My Mother Never Told Me

Cargoes are bartered, bought, sold and traded here. Sometimes a cargo with a specific destination is offloaded from one ship and onto another, thus freeing the first ship to return to its home port while the other ship continues on to the cargo's final destination, this saves time and money as well as enabling smaller carriers to compete in the lightyear's wide marketplace.

Cargoes that are offloaded are stored in the massive warehouse that lies beneath the actual parking field. Robots unload the ships and immediately transport the goods to the warehouse.

And that's where I come in. My job is to manage the warehouse. Mostly it is to supervise the robot cargo handlers and the few humans who work there as well. I also manage about a hundred cats, if you can call it management. Have you ever tried to herd cats? Can't be done.

The cats are there, of course, to catch and dispose of the various lifeforms such as rats, Karnian Suckers and the other small creatures that manage to enter the space ship's cargo holds. Without the cats Thevenin would be overrun by these vermin.

Stories My Mother Never Told Me

And the cats earn their keep. They roam the warehouse and the docks searching for their prey, and its mostly rats. But the cats also feed and water in specific places in the warehouse. Their food, in the feeding spots, is laced with birth control drugs which helps keep the population to a relatively small size. If that were not done the number of cats would far outnumber all the creatures that hitch rides on space ships and disembark here.

Now that I've told you all that "introductory" material I want to tell you about King Boots. I'll call him King for short. King, you see, somehow became attached to me. He got his name because he is coal black except for his white feet and the oddly shaped white spot on his head that resembles a crown. Kings wear crowns and so I named him King Boots. Very few of the cats have names but this one was special.

King would come by my office daily. He would purr and rub against my legs. Often, he would sleep on a small bed I had placed in the corner and his water bowl was always full. In return for my hospitality King would do his job.

Stories My Mother Never Told Me

And he would periodically prove that he was doing his job by bringing the body of a rat or Sucker, or other such animal to my office for me to approve. And then dispose of as well. I don't know how many of the captured creatures the cats actually completely ate. Their special food was consumed but not in great quantities, so it is my guess that they kept themselves properly fed as they moused around.

They really shouldn't be called mousers but ratters, because mice are actually rare here.

King is no longer around. I don't know what happened to him but I suspect that he was catnapped by the crew of a departing ship to help keep that ship's population of stowaways under control. And that's all right.

You see, King Boots had a way of capturing any number of different animals and would always present them to me, I guess to show what a great job he was doing. But then it began to get weird.

Rats and Suckers were common enough. But when ships from distant ports were here, King would bring strange prizes to me.

Stories My Mother Never Told Me

One time he dropped what looked like a very small dragon at my feet. It was scaly and had leathery wings, not unlike a bat's wings. But it definitely was not a bat. It was a lizard of some kind and I couldn't help but wonder whether it had breathed fire when it was still alive. King looked really proud of this capture.

But King's catches were becoming stranger and stranger. One time he brought me something that resembled a six-legged bird with a long rat-like tail. It had a beak in place of a mouth and, I kid you not, it was covered with feathers.

Now spaceport Thevenin has a fair number of birds. They have been here for almost as long as Thevenin has been under the dome. You see, Thevenin planet is airless and so the spaceport is protected by a massive dome structure. It is about two miles deep and close to that in width. It rises over three hundred feet to its highest point. When the dome was completed the administrator, at that time, introduced cats and birds to the environment.

Anyway. This, whatever it was, was not a bird by any stretch of the imagination. It didn't appear to have wings and six legs was way too many for any

Stories My Mother Never Told Me

bird I had ever seen. It was just it's beaked head and the feathers.

Then there was the time that King brought what looked like the cross between a featherless chicken and a crab. It had no discernable neck or head. It did have vestigial wings and a chicken like tail. It also had four legs with clawed feet. God knows where it came from. I'm almost glad that King couldn't talk or he would have told me where he found such a creature. I didn't want to know. Ships *were* coming from strange places. The thing is that I wasn't aware of the other cats making strange kills the way King Boots was. If they were, I would have heard.

And then there was the snake-like thing. It was about three feet long and looked, generally, like a snake. A snake with hair and very short non-functional legs. It had a huge head and mouth with fangs a good three inches long. How King killed it I'll never know. I was happy to dispose of that one.

I really began to wonder where King was finding these things. None of the other cats were harvesting anything close to King's strange finds. It

Stories My Mother Never Told Me

was almost like King Boots was entering another dimension to do his hunting.

The final straw came shortly before he disappeared. It was late in the day and I was getting ready to end my shift. I had been on the floor of the warehouse most of the day, supervising the robots and getting some specific containers organized to be loaded on a ship heading for Karnaugh.

I was in my office dictating my daily notes to the transcriber when King came in. I saw him from the corner of my eyes as he entered. I didn't pay much attention to him until I finished my notes. Then I turned and said, "What did you bring me this time?"

And I looked.

There, on the floor at my feet, was his latest kill. For a moment my heart stopped. It wasn't a malformed rat. It wasn't a mangled Sucker, or a bird or dragon.

It was a perfectly formed nude human being that was no more than nine inches tall. It was naked with a head of dark hair and a beard. I could see that

Stories My Mother Never Told Me

it was obviously male as it lay there on its back. It looked fit and muscular – and dead.

"Where did you get this, King?" I asked. But, of course, I got no answer.

For a few moments I just stared. I didn't know if I was seeing things or not. But I knew that it, whatever, or whoever, it was real, and dead, and on my office floor.

Suddenly I wasn't sure that I liked King Boots any more. I knew that I didn't like the gifts that he had been bring me for many weeks. In a moment of anger and disgust I chased him out of my office and shut the door. Then I stared at the little man on the floor.

"Where did you come from?" I asked. But, of course, he didn't answer. The other creatures that King Boots had brought me I unceremoniously dumped into the trash. But this one I could not. I didn't know what to do with it. Finally, I slid a piece of heavy plastic under the little body and lifted it. Then I slid it into a large envelope and sealed it.

Stories My Mother Never Told Me

I carried it with me as I left my office for the day. I placed it into the organic recyclables container near the exit and left the warehouse.

I took the next day off and searched the ways looking for any ship that could have carried anything like a little human but found nothing.

And I never saw King Boots again.

Stories My Mother Never Told Me

The Storm

Sometimes my best writing, as well as my worst, takes place at picnic tables in public parks. I sit at a table with my pen and tablet and write. It was a hot July day when I did exactly that and out came this little gem. All I knew, for sure about this story, was that I would use the line, "Thunder muttered in the hills..."

It was hot. It was always hot in Alabama in the summer. The heat index was over one hundred and the air was so thick that you could chew it. Thunder muttered in the hills. And the sky in the southwest was darkening. He knew it was going to be a long night. But perversely he loved storms, especially thunderstorms with madly flashing lightening and thunder that never seemed to stop. He could watch all night.

The sky was the color of beaten copper, dull and motionless. The air at ground level was the color he loved for outdoor nature photography. The color of the air, if there was such a thing, was a kind of dull greenish-brass; clear as crystal. Not a leaf moved in the trees bordering his property. Everything stood out is sharp detail. The depth of

128

Stories My Mother Never Told Me

his view was astounding, it seemed that he was looking at a View master slide rather than real life.

The thunder was coming closer as it rolled and rumbled through the low hills. Without warning, a wind rushed through the trees and the stillness was broken like a stone shattering a mirror. It was the outflow from the leading edge of the coming storm. He had learned that through experience and by studying weather forecasting.

The wind howled and the trees bent to its power. Leaves torn from twigs and branches filled the air like a green summer snow. A branch broke from a tall tree and slammed into the earth. The wind screamed in the eaves of the roof and the very house shook in the gale.

And, as quickly as it came, it ceased. The sudden stillness was almost deafening in its silence. Once again, the world was like a still painting or photograph.

The thunder no longer muttered. It was mumbling and beginning to shout imprecations; at the sky? at the earth? at the very storm cell that brought it to life?

Stories My Mother Never Told Me

The copper and brass, through an unknown alchemy, transmuted into iron and then lead as the sky darkened and the world became as night.

'This is going to be a really bad one.' He thought. A blinding flash of lightening lit the room in which he was standing – the sunroom. Everything stood out in stark detail as though it was being photographed in the brightness of the flash. Spots danced before his eyes.

"One thousand and one, one thousand and two, one thousand and three," he intoned. He got all the way to one thousand and seven before he heard the peal thunder. A mile and a half away. It was then that the sirens began to wail.

He turned on the television.

A weather map appeared on the screen showing the radar signature of the storms. A huge bloom of deep red loomed not far from where he lived. It was just a part of a string of storms crossing from the neighboring state of Mississippi and that was originating even farther to the southwest in Arkansas.

'It's going to be a long night,' he thought.

Stories My Mother Never Told Me

And then, as though it had leapt across the intervening miles, it was upon him. Lightening flashed and the simultaneous report of sharp flat thunder shook the windows and the house, before rolling down the bowling alley that was the valley in which he lived.

He poured himself a glass of whisky and said out loud, "I might as well get ready."

He went into his bedroom and took off all his clothes. He folded them neatly and placed them on the bed. He returned to the sunroom. He stood at the glass door, watching the storm assail the back yard and the fields beyond. The tall grass of the field was laid flat.

The rain began. Not a gentle pattering on the roof but instead, it was like tremendous buckets upended and dumping their contents all at once, then righting to be filled again. The deafening sound the rain made on the roof drowned out all other sounds. If the sirens were still blowing, they could not be heard. Even the weatherman on the television mouthed silently to the camera as he stood in front of the green screen.

He stood at the glass door and watched.

Stories My Mother Never Told Me

'This time,' he thought as he sipped his whisky, 'this time I *will* get one. I have to. And it will prove, once and for all, that they *are* real.' He racked a bullet into the chamber of his pistol and checked the safety. Then he put the gun on the small table by the door – within easy and fast reach.

And he waited.

He raised his glass to his lips but sipped nothing from the empty glass. He quickly went to the liquor cabinet and poured himself another and once again took his sentry position by the door. Only the glass separating him from the wrath of the elements.

And he watched.

The storm poured its rage onto the earth. It lashed everything with rain. And then the hail came. The stones bounced in the grass and beat a tattoo on the windows and roof. Then everything was still. The lawn was covered with leaves and small tree branches. The hailstones glowed in the unearthly light. But the calm was false – and he knew it.

Lightening flashed and the sharp bang of the accompanying thunder rattled the windows, shook the house and reverberated in his chest. It felt as

Stories My Mother Never Told Me

though all the air had been sucked out of the house and his lungs. The lights flickered and darkness fell upon the earth. It was then that he saw the first one.

It was a male and stood, perhaps, five feet tall. It was totally nude and its skin was a pale greyish color. The – whatever it was – had a pointed head and a hooked nose that grew from its face in a Pinocchioish fashion. The creature danced and waved its arms and kicked its feet high into the air. Its ridiculously long phallus swung between its legs. It took that piece of flesh in its hand and flipped it to and fro as it danced. A horrible lascivious grin widened its mouth literally from ear to ear.

With its free hand it waved "come out! Come out and dance with me."

But he stood behind the protection of the glass door and watched; whisky in one hand and the pistol in the other.

While he had been distracted by the first creature, others materialized and began to dance in the yard. They were lit by flashes of lightening and the thunder beat a strange and hellish rhythm for their stamping feet. In moments they formed a circle around the first creature – he hesitated to name

Stories My Mother Never Told Me

them – and danced their macabre ring-around-the-rosie. Circling faster and faster around the well-endowed creature in the center.

In the flashing lightening and pouring rain they danced, beckoning him to leave the safety of his home to join them. They opened a place in the circle and urged him to come and join in the hellish rain drenched dance.

By now there must have been twenty of them cavorting in his back yard. Dancing to a tune only they could hear. Twenty in a circle, stamping their feet into the wet grass. As they stamped, he could see the water splashing upward into the air.

They weren't all male. At least half were female, their pendulous breasts flopping on their chests and bellies. While they danced the males bent low, their hands actually dragged on the ground. If they were chanting, they could not be heard through the thunder, wind and rain. Though they surely looked like they were directing their incantations into the dark skies.

Now the females pulled from the circle and facing him in a macabre chorus line, danced

Stories My Mother Never Told Me

lasciviously, grinning and contorting their bodies in crude sexual poses.

Behind them the males danced in a line as well, jumping and leaping high into the air, waving their arms and stamping their feet. Then the leader stepped through the lines and in an obscene dance invited him to join in their cavorting fun.

He put down his whisky and put the pistol's safety on fire. He opened the door and stepped outside into the storm. He approached the creatures as they stomped and cheered his approach. He felt the wet grass squish beneath his feet.

The leader waved to and beckoned the approaching man.

As he approached the dancing creatures he looked down. His feet were long and broad and flat. To his horror he could see his skinny legs and his distended belly. He could see his own member swinging between his legs!

He approached the leader and raised the gun.

'I've got you now,' he thought.

Stories My Mother Never Told Me

The flash of lightening, the peal of thunder and the single gunshot took place at exactly the same instant. And the lightening revealed that there was nothing in the yard.

The storms passed and the next day his neighbors found his nude body lying in his yard – dead – with a single gunshot wound to the heart.

Stories My Mother Never Told Me

Murder Most Rare

*Thevenin Spaceport is a place where I have spent many years writing stories that never saw the light of day, literally. To this day, I make up stories to help me sleep, or pass the time during those sleepless nights, you've already read two. **Murder Most Rare** came to me recently and I wrote most of it as I lay in bed at night. So, it was easy one to transfer to paper. On Thevenin murder is most rare.*

Part I
Welcome to Thevenin, Crossroads of the Stars

One of my favorite places is to simply sit in my office balcony and look over the widespread and varied Thevenin Spaceport. From the height of about three hundred feet, I can see almost the entire spaceport, from the field to the living complex to the casino and everything in between.

Who am I? My name is Richard Matieson and I'm the Administrator of Spaceport Thevenin. This

Stories My Mother Never Told Me

is my domain. If anything, you could call me a benevolent dictator. The spaceport is a business and the people who live here, for the greater part, work for me. In exchange I provide excellent housing, food, entertainment, working hours and benefits. But more of that later.

Some two miles from my balcony is the shield wall, through which the one-of-a-kind ship port extends into the vacuum of the planet's surface. Planet Thevenin has no atmosphere and probably never did. So why a spaceport on an airless planet? That has everything to do with Chalmers Jump Points.

But before I tell you about that, a little more about the spaceport, *then* why it exists. The spaceport itself is protected by a huge, squat, Quonset; a half-round structure that is approximately two miles long, a mile wide and a little over three hundred feet in height. The side walls are rather steep instead of being rounded, to allow for more living and working space.

The Quonset, for the most part, is covered with a structure composed of large quartz panels which allow the sunlight to shine through. The

Stories My Mother Never Told Me

quartz has a UV limiting coating. It allows an amount of ultra violet light equal to that which your average planetary atmosphere filters. This good for both our greenery as well as our sun loving population. The Quonset is reinforced to contain the pressure of the atmosphere pressing against the quartz panels. This structure also is used as internal infrastructure for rain making, lighting and more.

The largest portion of the spaceport is the field. The field runs about one and three quarters miles deep out to the shield wall, and is about half a mile wide. It is here where space ships themselves are birthed while in port. It can support about three hundred ships, though we rarely have more than two hundred in port at any given time.

Assuming that the field is oriented to the east/west cardinal points then, to the south, is the living area. Here are apartments, we call them apts, enough to house sixty thousand persons. Along with the housing there are various food stores, department stores, schools (though virtual schooling would save space and resources, it is a known fact that human interaction is a vital part of the learning experience) arcades, clubs, restaurants and much more. Much of this space is dug into the southern crater wall. There is a tunnel that extends south into another rather small crater. This crater is domed and contains what we call the forest – a nice stand of varied trees composed of evergreens and hard woods. This is a very popular space that the population treats with great respect while, at the same time, uses for their enjoyment. It also acts as an excellent air filtration system, and low maintenance at that.

Just to the north, between the living area and the field is an open space with a small lake, beach, picnic area, playing fields and the like. This is called the Park and it is used daily by everyone, including myself.

To the west, also dug into the crater wall, is the administrative area. Often called the City, this is where the hospital, library, museums, symphony and opera and so much more, as well as the administrative seat of government reside. This is where my office is located. Outside companies also have offices in this area. Out front is a wide Plaza that extends the full mile from south to north. Here are more restaurants and small shops that cater to the tourists who visit Thevenin on their way to other places.

Stories My Mother Never Told Me

Beneath the Plaza which sits between the administrative area and the field is the warehouse. The warehouse extends the width of the field, about half a mile, the floor is level with the field's birthing area. The warehouse extends back some three hundred feet under the Plaza and is about fifty feet high. That's almost 40 million cubic feet of storage. The "workers" are all robots which are supervised by a small team of humans. The robots unload ships and transport the cargo to the warehouse where it is carefully catalogued and stored in long aisles and racks of shelves. They also transport cargo to ships and load their holds. Sometimes robots are used to transload two ships. Transloading is the shifting of cargo between ships as they swap cargoes.

To the north, standing free from the cliff wall is The Hotel. There are actually two hotels in Thevenin but this one is called The Hotel. It's actually operated by Hilton but as the first here it bears the distinction of *The Hotel*.

Built high into the north wall is the Casino. This is also a hotel, built and operated by the Authority, it sports the only casino here and is heavily visited by tourists, more so than the local

Stories My Mother Never Told Me

population. The nighttime view from here is quite spectacular.

Extending along the base of the northern cliff wall is the hydroponics farm and protein factory. The term "factory" was given many years ago and has stuck, though it bears little semblance to a traditional factory. It is here where meat, such as beef, lamb, chicken and pork are raised. No actual animals are involved but the meats that are grown here were once cultured from living animals. Here also is where "seafood" is raised. The same process is used to generate various fish species but clams, oysters, some fish species, and shrimp are actually raised live on premises.

Hydroponics is multistoried, as is the factory, where most of the produce is raised. This building stands three hundred feet high, one thousand feet long and three hundred feet wide. Again, the factory has roughly the same dimensions. Much food is also shipped to Thevenin in stasis containers. This method keeps the consumables, mostly fruits and vegetables fresh until they are stored locally and consumed.

Stories My Mother Never Told Me

Beyond the factory are various maintenance and other facilities for keeping the infrastructure operating.

Running around the periphery of the field, including housing and the factory area is the Slider. The Slider stands some twenty feet above the Plaza and borders the field. The Slider is a people mover composed of three parallel moving conveyors, running at speeds up to ten miles per hour. The outermost runs at two mph while the next inward runs at six and, of course, the innermost at ten. From an early age, riders learn how to move from one conveyor to the next. The Slider runs out and back with "stations" placed every thousand feet or so. This permits people to exit down to the Plaza level or cross over to travel in the opposite direction, or disembark at various production facilities.

On the north, sandwiched between the facilities previously discussed and the Slider, are the Bazaar and the Underground.

The Bazaar is a kind of free for all shop complex which artists and crafts people tender their trades to the public. You can buy almost anything there and all the shops are owned and operated by

Stories My Mother Never Told Me

locals. No outsiders allowed. It's a great place to visit. There is even a small distillery there. Makes good whiskey.

The Underground is a converted water reservoir. When new ones were dug a couple of hundred of years ago, this one was converted into a six-story shopping mall. The lowest level of which supports a large holodeck – a very popular attraction. The shops and stores here again are used mostly by tourists, though the local population shops here as well, but the prices are higher here than in the shops in the residential part of the spaceport. But then the tourists don't know about them.

Between the Underground and the field is the terminal. This juts out into the field about a thousand feet and is so situated to allow up to four ships to berth to permit passengers to exit or board the ships. Here passage may also be purchased. When passenger ships berth here, in normal circumstances, the majority of passengers disembark and take up temporary residence at the hotel or casino. And they gamble like crazy! Sometimes the hotel rooms are a part of their transport, or tour, package, sometimes it's extra. Either way they are happy to get off the ship for a

Stories My Mother Never Told Me

while. Space travel, in reality, can be very boring and confining.

Now. As to why there is a spaceport on an airless planet. There are only two other planets in this system and they are both gas giants far from the principal – obviously not inhabitable. Thevenin is approximately one hundred million miles from the sun and is nothing but an airless dirtball. So why a spaceport?

When Thevenin was founded, there were three Chalmers Jump Points close by. The nearest only three weeks travel distant. They all follow the planet in its orbit. Since those days, two more points have been discovered, thus making Thevenin the Crossroads of the Stars. More spaceships pass through our ship lock than any other spaceport in the cloud. Our LTOF system launches and lands nearly fifty ships a day. That's nearly two every hour. To say the least that keeps our traffic control team busy.

For those readers that don't know about Chalmers Jump Points here is a very brief summary of what they are.

Stories My Mother Never Told Me

Surprisingly, nobody knows how they work. Our best guess is that they are wormholes leading to other points of the cloud and one to the Milky Way Galaxy itself. They provide almost instantaneous travel from the entry point to its exit. Imagine traveling from the mother galaxy itself to the smaller Magellanic Cloud in an instant. Now that's moving.

I'm not going to give a history of Chalmers Jump Points here, that's for another time and place. Just believe me that ships come and go through those points in this vicinity more than anywhere else. It is worth noting that the largest number of Chalmers Jump Points anywhere else is only three. So, from Thevenin a ship can travel to almost anywhere in no time – that is in space travel time.

Stories My Mother Never Told Me

Part II
The Administrator

Let me to properly reintroduce myself. Again, my name is Richard Matieson CFR RSA[2]. Most people call me Rich, I am the administrator of Thevenin Spaceport, in other words, I'm the boss, of everything. But I'm also a really nice guy.

My office is on the top floor of the Administration building in the west cliff wall. And that's where my balcony is. And that's where I do much of my "office" work. The balcony will easily seat six people and I often have meetings there. From here I can watch ships arrive and leave, see people on the Slider and much more.

The way I operate is that my office is usually quiet. I see sales people – we just can't get rid of the travelling salesman, meet with the board of directors, of which I am the chair, work on planning sessions and the like. The actual operation of the spaceport I let my division leads run. Each has her

---

[2] CFM: Certified Fleet Manager. RSA: Registered Spaceport Administrator

Stories My Mother Never Told Me

or his own area of expertise and can run the division much better than I could.

The spaceport authority is composed of the following divisions

• **Agriculture**: Management of the hydroponic farms as well as engineered meat, fowl and fish – the Factory

• **Business Administration**: The actual daily operation of the spaceport including the all-important collection of landing and takeoff fees as well as demurrage

• **City Management**: The handling of all aspects of daily life for the average citizen from housing to shopping, entertainment, etc.

• **Energy**: Including power generation and storage

• **Environment**: Management of fresh air and water as well as waste treatment and recycling

• **Maintenance**: Comprising the physical plant and infrastructure maintenance and construction

Stories My Mother Never Told Me

- **Security**: A security force assigned to maintain the peace among the citizens and visitors, incoming and outgoing security and customs

- **Traffic Control**: The vital group that keeps spaceships moving into and out of the protected area, landing and takeoff of ships, birth management, orbital management and safety

Every morning I hold a meeting with all my division heads. The ideal is to attend in person but sometimes a member or two must appear virtually via a Holo link. The only way you can tell they are not physically present is that their desktops don't match my conference room tabletop.

It's then that we all discuss what is happening through the spaceport. These meetings keep all informed of what is happening on other divisions. We call these meetings scrums. It is also in these meetings that I mete out assignments as well as follow important things happening throughout the system.

Today was one of those days. The meeting started at 9:30 as all scrums do. Everyone was present and we shared small talk for a few minutes before I started the discussion.

Stories My Mother Never Told Me

"Scott," I said. "What's the news from Traffic Control?"

"Well, right now, we have one hundred twenty-seven ships in port. We're expecting twelve in and five out today, six have already arrived and none have left." We don't have anything stacked up, though we are expecting a passenger ship of about five-hundred in about a month. That's it."

I nodded to Phil Mercherson of Maintenance.

"Not much today. We're going to do some preventative maint on one of the roller bearings in the Slider but it won't affect the riders. They won't even know."

And so around the room until I got to Carol Berks of Environment.

"We have a problem," she said.

"And what's that?"

"We're going to have to shut down reservoir number two for a while."

I interrupted, "how long?"

Stories My Mother Never Told Me

"I don't know yet. We have to find out what is contaminating it. We've already shut down the cross links between one and three and so no contamination has spread. What we know right now is that there is some kind of biologic contamination in two. It's low level but we have to remove it."

"Any idea of what it is?"

"It might be something that got passed in from recycling that shouldn't have. We're checking on it. Six-million gallons of water is a lot to deal with. Once we find and remove the contaminant, it's still going to take a few days to disinfect the water. It looks like a week before we'll have it up and running."

"Keep me closely posted on your progress. But tanks one and three are OK?"

"Yes," Carol replied. "We're keeping a close eye on them and they are fine and are full as well."

"Like I said, please keep me posted." I turned to the next in line and continued the meeting.

Later as I was working on the balcony, I got a call from Carol Berks.

Stories My Mother Never Told Me

"Boss, I think you ought to get down here to tank two. You have to see this."

"I'm on my way."

The reservoirs are buried deep in the rock of the planet and are isolated. They receive the purified water that comes from recycling. On Thevenin we recycle everything that can possibly be recycled and that means a lot. There are three reservoirs in the system. Each holds six million gallons. That may sound like a lot of water, combining three tanks. Eighteen million should last quite a while. But hydroponics takes a large cut as does rain.

Every part of the spaceport gets rain at least once a week. It keeps down the dust and anything else that is airborne, sweetens the air and keeps all the greenery watered – and there is a lot of greenery. The birds like it as well. The rains rotate through the various zones on a daily basis and no part gets unwashed. Interestingly enough, the spaceport is large enough to generate its own weather, so sometimes there are small clouds and it actually rains on its own – but we don't depend on it.

I quickly left my office and took the bounce tube to the ground floor. Then I walked to the Slider

Stories My Mother Never Told Me

and took it to the exit nearest the Factory where the entrance to the underground system was located. I scanned my card at the door and went down the short ramp to the entrance of recycling and water purification.

These two locations were isolated from each other except for the purification tanks which allowed the clean and potable water to pass. Here it was that the water also received its share of minerals to restore the taste and Ph balance so that the water didn't taste flat. From here the water flowed into the reservoirs.

I followed the hallway to tank two and found Carol and a number of other people standing at the rail of the tank.

"What have you got?" I asked.

"Trouble. That's what we have. Maybe lots of it!" She paused. "We have an ROV down at the bottom of the tank now. Look at what it found."

She pointed to the Holo that the operator was watching to guide the under-water robot. There in the ROV's cameras was lighted – a human body.

"Holy fuck," I muttered.

Stories My Mother Never Told Me

"Exactly," was Carol's reply. "This really makes everything worse. Not only do we have a bigger disinfection process, but we have to find a way to get that...that *thing* out of there."

"We can pull up the rover and attach a grapple to it. We can lower it back down and maybe it can grab onto the body." Said the ROV operator.

"But that runs the chance that it might become dismembered. We don't know how long it has been down there. It might fall apart. Then we'll have an even bigger mess."

One of the techs spoke up. "Can we lower something like a tarp with some drain holes cut into it and roll the body onto it and the pull that up manually. That might be a lot safer."

Another nodded, "That might work."

The robot operator said, "You'll need more than that. Look, there are weights tied to the body. You'll need something strong."

Everyone peered into the Holo and could clearly see that the body was encumbered at the arms, legs and torso with some kind of weights. Bringing it up wasn't going to be easy.

Stories My Mother Never Told Me

Carol said, "We're gonna have to use the repair sub to get hold of that. I think we have no other choice."

"How long will that take?" I asked.

"At least an hour just to get it here. After that, I have no idea. But at least it has the appendages to handle the job."

"Well, get it moving," I said.

She nodded and turned to one of her techs to get the job started. I turned and spoke to my aid. "Better call security and get security down here, maybe a detective, just in case. And get the medical examiner as well." He spoke into his headset and nodded to me. And then we waited.

It took an hour until the sub arrived. It was encapsulated in its own little truck with a crane on the back. The driver turned and backed the truck so that the crane was poised at the water's edge. The driver jumped from the open cab and asked what the job was.

Quickly he was brought up to speed and he started the crane and lifted the sub and placed it into

Stories My Mother Never Told Me

the water. He climbed into the vessel and released it from the hooks of the crane.

"Radio check," he called over the communications channel.

"Loud and clear," was the response. With that he maneuvered the sub out into the open water. Soon bubbles flooded around as it quickly sank into the depths.

Just then both the medical examiner and the detective arrived. The detective, speaking for both, showed his badge and said, "who's in charge and why are we here?"

Carol said, "I am. I'm Carol Berks, head of the Environmental Division. We have a human body at the bottom of the tank. It looks like it was weighted down before it went into the water. It looks suspicious."

"To say the least. I'm chief detective Jim Caputo. This is Medical Examiner Bill Flood. We'll watch and wait."

We all watched and waited as the sub slowly reached the bottom of the reservoir tank.

Stories My Mother Never Told Me

Finally, we heard the operator say, "I'm here. Looks like someone had it out for this guy, he's practically wrapped in these weights."

We all turned to watch the sub's Holo. Slowly and carefully the arms extended from the sub and reached for the body. They gently slid beneath the body and carefully rocked up and back, thus holding the body in place.

"Got it," he said. "I'm on my way up."

"Make sure there is nothing left down there before you move," Carol almost shouted.

"Roger that," came the laconic reply.

And then we waited for the sub to surface. After about twenty minutes it did. Once on the surface the operator carefully came to the edge and extended the arms and body out over the concrete edging. The Medical Examiner and his two assistants moved to disentangle the body from the sub's arms. The weights clanked as the body was lowered. A stretcher was pushed under the sub's arms and the body was deposited on it.

"Get this up to my lab," the ME told his assistants. "Cover it and keep out of the public eye."

Stories My Mother Never Told Me

He turned to me and the detective, "Looks like murder to me. I can't imagine anyone tying themselves up like that and then jumping into the water. No way." He shook his head, turned and began to follow his assistants.

Part III
Murder in Thevenin

I turned from the Medical Examiner and said to the administrator, "I'll take it from here. If this is murder, and it surely does look like it, I'll need to talk with everyone involved and then some.

Administrator Matieson told me, "Do what you have to do. But, if you can, keep it quiet. Murder is most rare on Thevenin. I don't know when we had the last one."

"Don't worry. I know how to do my job and how to keep it quiet." The administrator nodded as I turned and followed Bill Flood, the ME. But I wouldn't talk with, or see, him until the next morning.

Stories My Mother Never Told Me

My name is James Caputo. Most people call me either Cap or sir. Very few call me Jim – I don't like it. I'm the chief of detectives of Thevenin Spaceport Security. Of course, I'm only one of three crime detectives in the security force. Customs has a couple of detectives as well. And there are two investigators in the security detachment in the field but if anything, even a little difficult or out of line comes along, it's my team that they call.

To be honest, I've never investigated a murder before. In fact, I checked the records and the last murder on Thevenin happened over a hundred years ago! It is most rare, as the administrator said.

It looked like I would really have to brush up my investigative skills. I was going to need them.

The next morning, I went to the Medical Examiner's office. I knew Bill Flood but had never had to work this closely with him before. Mostly we played golf out at the Cliffs course.

"Morning, Cap. How's your day."

"Up to now, not bad," I grinned. "What do you have for me?"

Stories My Mother Never Told Me

"It looks like murder all right. This poor guy took a vibroblade to the back. Nearly cut his heart in two. He was dead before he hit the floor."

"What can you tell me about him?"

"Not much at the moment. There were no personal effects on him. All I can say is that he is a male, approximately thirty-five years old and in good shape. But no ID. I sent off a sample for DNA, so hopefully we'll know who he is – or was – in a couple of hours. I requested that the information be sent to you as well as myself. I'd guess that he was in the water for three or four days."

"And we've been drinking that! Could he have gone in on Friday?" I asked. "And, just to let you know, the administrator doesn't want to let word to get out about this until we know what happened so let's keep this close."

"Same here. Want to take a look? He was really trussed up. Look." Bill turned the now nude body on its back and pointed to the arms first. "You can see ligature marks where he was tied. And they were tight, rope by the looks of it, quarter inch rope, available just about anywhere. The same around his legs," he pointed. "And his torso as well. There were

160

Stories My Mother Never Told Me

ten-pound weights on his arms and legs and two fives around his torso. That much weight would easily have pulled him to the bottom. Yes, he definitely did not tie himself up and jump off. Besides, there was no water in his lungs. Dead people don't drown, you know.

"And here are the weights." He pointed to the pile on the adjacent table. "As you can see, they are standard gym lifting weights."

"But at least they are a clue." I said, "I do have somewhere to start. Surely the gyms and clubs will know whether there are missing weights."

"Yes," Bill said, "Unless, of course, the murderer owned them himself. Then nobody would miss them."

"Thanks for the cold shower." I sourly replied. "Here I thought I had my case solved. Looks like I'll have to actually do some detecting."

"Well, good luck."

I turned and returned to my desk – you could hardly call it an office – to think. My first question, of course, was where to start.

Stories My Mother Never Told Me

I'd take a chance. "ALURA, are there any reports of gyms reporting missing or stolen lifting weights?"

ALURA responded, "Let me check." It's sweet contralto voice always makes me forget that she is only a computer interface. But she does know me better than anyone else.

Almost instantly she said, "I can't find anything. Let me check farther back than a year." A brief pause, "nothing."

"Ok, thanks."

ALURA is an interface to the spaceport computer network. It, though I call it she, is a part of me, settled right behind my right ear. She "speaks" to me by cochlear implant. She 'hears' what I say by both subvocalization or when I speak aloud. She is smart enough to know when I am addressing her specifically as opposed to generally speaking. If she intercepts words or phrases in a conversation, from either party, that are germane to what she and I may have been discussing, she may talk to me and provide information that I might need. I don't know how I ever got along without her.

Stories My Mother Never Told Me

There was little that I could do for a number of hours but finally, late in the afternoon, I got word about the victim. His name was Peter Spence and he had worked in the warehouse that served the field. Because it was too late in the day to pursue information in the warehouse itself, I put that task off for the morrow. By now, I was ready to call it a day.

The next morning, Wednesday, I took myself down to the warehouse. I left my office in the administrative section and rode the slider to the southern station, near the park. There I took a ramp that curved round to the warehouse floor, some sixty feet below the Plaza level. There, along the western wall was a block of offices. After entering I looked for and found the reception desk. A robot was stationed there. I spoke to it asking for the manager. It directed me to a block of offices not far from where I was standing.

"What is the manager's name?" I asked

"Ms. Candice Potter" was the reply.

I walked to the manager's office and entered. There a human receptionist asked my business. I showed her my badge. "I'm detective Caputo with

Stories My Mother Never Told Me

the spaceport security service and I need to speak with Ms. Potter."

She spoke to her computer, looked up to me and said, "Just go down that hall and take the third door to the left."

I thanked her and went down the hall, there were no doors to the right because that wall was all glass looking out onto the warehouse floor. It was quite an amazing sight. I found the door, knocked and entered. A rather young woman looked up from her work.

"Ms. Potter?" I asked.

She smiled, which made her face radiant, "I'm Candy Potter. You must be detective Caputo. Have a seat." She pointed to the chair facing her desk, "What can I do for you?"

"Thank you for seeing me. What can you tell me about Peter Spence. I understand that he works for you."

She thought for a moment, "Yes, I can tell you about Pete. He's one of our top supervisors. He is the team lead for about fifteen managers and has his own crew as well."

Stories My Mother Never Told Me

"Does he do a good job?"

"Yes, in fact he's up for a promotion. He's one of our best." She smiled.

"When was the last time you saw him, or when he last worked?"

"He was on leave last week. I heard that he was staying at the cliffs, so he probably worked the last time the week before last." She began to have a puzzled and concerned look to her face. "Why do you ask?"

I didn't know how to put it to her without revealing too much so I simply said, "I'm sorry but he died about five days ago and I'm trying to look back to learn whether anyone noticed how he looked or if he acted as though he was ill." It sounded so lame.

She looked shocked, of course, and breathed inward sharply, her lips parted revealing perfect white teeth. As she shook her head her blonde hair formed a halo around her face.

"Oh no! He was one of our best and such a nice man. Everyone liked him and he went out of his way to help... everyone. What happened?"

Stories My Mother Never Told Me

I had to come clean with her. "This is confidential so please keep all that I tell you to yourself and I apologize for being so vague. It looks like someone killed him. That's why I'm here. It's my job to find out who and why. At the moment we have no clues and no indication as to why someone would want to kill him – but it happened. I'm hoping that I can learn something here."

"This is so hard to believe. Who could do something like that to such a good man? I don't know what to tell you. You can examine his work records but I don't think you'll find anything."

"What kind of hours did he work?" I asked.

"Mostly the day shift, but I know that he did rotate with others once in a while to work one of the overnight shifts if someone needed to trade. He didn't have a family, so I guess it didn't matter to him when he worked."

"Do you mind if I look around?"

"Go right ahead, but watch the red lines on the floor. The robots will avoid you but it's always safest to stay in the human lanes. Oh yes, and get

Stories My Mother Never Told Me

earplugs and safety glasses when you enter the warehouse floor. Safety first, you know."

So, I thanked her and left the office block. When I entered the warehouse floor, I made sure that I took the precautions Ms. Potter gave me. I had a general idea of how large the warehouse area was but I was still astounded as its size. It was brightly lit and extended into the distance. Robots rolled here and there, some pushing carts loaded with goods bound for who knows where while others carried containers.

Pillars rose to the roof, some fifty feet above the floor. At each of these pillars was a desk. At some of them people sat or stood, monitoring Holo feeds of the work in their assigned areas. I didn't actually see any humans interacting with robots but could see one or two apparently speaking to the Holos. I approached the nearest desk.

As I did so the man seated there looked up. "Something you need?"

He didn't look happy to see me, so I showed him my badge and introduced myself. His attitude immediately changed. "Do you know Peter Spence?" I asked.

Stories My Mother Never Told Me

"Yeah, I know Pete. Not very well because he isn't in my sector but I run into him once in a while."

"Nice guy?"

"Yeah, I guess. Like I said…"

"Ok, so where does he work? Where is *his* sector?"

"Oh, it's down that way," he pointed. "About a quarter mile, in the blue sector. The posts, er the desks, will be blue."

It looked like quite a hike. I turned and began the trek when the man said, "Stay inside the red lines."

Yeah, I knew. In an area that large it seemed to take forever to walk to the blue sector but it really only took a couple of minutes. In the blue sector every workstation or desk was blue, as were the pillars. It was then that I noticed that the entire warehouse was color coded. The racks for goods were all blue in this sector. I looked back and noted that the sector I had just left was red. Off to my left I could see what had to be the yellow sector.

Stories My Mother Never Told Me

I didn't see anyone at first but finally I spied someone standing at a desk and so I went to that place, minding the red lines on the floor, of course. Robots whizzed past me going in all directions. The whole warehouse was like that – controlled madness. I came up to the woman standing at the desk and watched her working with a Holo, talking into it but also using some kind of hand motions – or maybe they were signals. As I stepped up to her I could see that she was aware of me, so I stood silently until she had the time to turn to me.

"May I help you sir?" she asked.

"I'm sorry to interrupt you but I have a few questions I'd like to ask." I showed her my badge.

She nodded, "I have a couple of minutes, two or three."

"Thank you. Do you work for Peter Spence?"

She nodded, "Yes, he is my supervisor on the shifts that we work together."

"Is that often?"

"Yes, we usually work the same shift unless he has to work at night, but that isn't often."

Stories My Mother Never Told Me

"Is he a good man to work for?"

"Just about the best," she said. I could see by her name tag that she was called Cindy.

I asked her, "When was the last time you saw him?"

"It was the week before last, on Friday, at quitting time. He said he was going to take some time off and to go to the Cliffs to play golf over the weekend. Why? Is he OK?" She frowned at the last.

"I'm sorry, but he was killed in an accident. I'm just tying up loose ends."

Her eyes quickly filled with tears and she wiped them with the back of her hand. "I'm sorry," she sniffed. "He was such a good man. I really liked him. What happened?"

"I can't tell you that just yet but I know that he didn't suffer. Does he have a desk or workstation in this sector?"

She pointed, "Down that way about four or five posts. You can't miss it because there is a sign that says, 'Super' over it."

Stories My Mother Never Told Me

I thanked her and walked in the direction where she pointed. I heard her call, "Watch the red lines," as I walked away. They took this safety-first stuff seriously. Just then a juggernaut of a robot whooshed past me at what looked like a breakneck speed. This wasn't like any of the robots I had seen by now. This one stood at least five feet tall and about ten feet long. It was pulling a train of carriages, all loaded to the brim. Had it hit me it would have left my mangled body in its wake. I definitely would pay more attention from now on in. It was soon followed by another and then a third. Later I learned that there were even more of them, all carting cargo to a ship that was loading out in the field.

I safely got to Spence's post. It was actually a tall desk with a Holo tank on the top surface and it was lined with drawers. There were a few papers on the top but none were of any interest to me. They all seemed to be notations regarding where things were stocked, which aisle, rack and level. I rummaged through the drawers but didn't find anything meaningful, that is until I got the bottom most one. It was locked but Ms. Potter had given me a temporary pass card that should open it.

Stories My Mother Never Told Me

I passed the card over the lock and the drawer sprang open. In it were a number of papers. I pulled them out and placed them on the desktop. Most of them were hand written copies of time keeping records, notes about people working for him and the like. But one caught my attention, simply because it was so different in content from the rest.

Along the top it had a red border and the caption read, "*Starways Freight Carriers*" The second line read, "*Bill of Lading*." Beneath that was a table of what appeared to be goods to be stored in the warehouse. One line was highlighted.

It said, "**Neuro TRX MET (MICETD) Implant, Qty 5, TX5056B74281**"

I didn't know what it was but it looked like Spence was paying attention to it. I spoke to ALURA, "Babe, what can you tell me about this?" And I read the line to her.

"It doesn't sound familiar but I'll keep looking. I'll let you know when I find something."

That was unusual, ALURA could almost instantly find anything. I flashed the form and put everything back into the drawer and locked it. I

Stories My Mother Never Told Me

figured that I had all that I could find here. Carefully I skirted the red lines back to the warehouse office block. And from there I went back to the surface. Once in the Plaza, I stopped for a bite to eat before returning to my desk.

Once at my desk I queried ALURA again. I asked, "Can you identify TX5056B74281, Neuro TRX MET (MICETD)?"

Almost immediately she said, "This is an implantable neural transmitter/receiver manufactured by the BioLogic Corporation headquartered on Karnaugh. Its primary use is to receive programming from an external source, interpret the data and deliver impulses to the appropriate part of the human nervous system, as needed. It is a therapeutic device. Would you like me to read you the manual?"

"No thanks, sweety, what does look like? Can you find an image"

Almost immediately a Holo sprang to life before me showing a small disk about half an inch across. "That's it?" I asked.

Stories My Mother Never Told Me

"That is the device. It is programmed externally, after it has been implanted."

"What's it used for?"

"My research indicates that the device is used for numerous treatments. For example, it can ease pain and tremors. It has been used to treat nervous disorders. As well as control of some glandular secretions and hormones.

"It is implanted into the patient at a location within the body where it's signals will have an effect on the diagnosed problem. Once it is implanted, it is externally programmed and is thereafter autonomous."

"Is it expensive?"

"Very. It is not frequently used and is mostly a last resort. A single unit will cost about 100,000□."

"Ouch! Anything else?"

"It can be hacked."

"Do tell me more."

"It can be hacked and reprogrammed beyond its set parameters. Doing so violates the warranty

Stories My Mother Never Told Me

and can turn it into a highly and permanently addictive cerebral neural stimulator. In other words, it can be attached to the brain stem and can affect the pleasure centers of the brain; to the extent that it is usually fatal within a few months but the victim dies happy. Often, when this happens, the device is removed, sterilized and reimplanted – for a price, of course."

"Is that why Peter Spence was interested in it? Could it be that he was going to steal one, or the entire shipment, and resell it?" With that thought the next step for me was to examine his apt. It was located in residential J-4#5.

I hopped on the Slider and was whisked away to the residential section. There I entered the management office and spoke to the manager on duty. I showed her my badge and requested access to Spence's apt. Access was granted and directions given. I took the jump tube to the tenth floor and found corridor Four. Apt 5 was just down the hall and used my newly acquired pass key to enter.

I went in and found a neatly kept living space. There were two bedrooms, one outfitted as a home office and library, a living space and kitchenette.

Stories My Mother Never Told Me

There was a view of the forest courtesy of a HoloWall. Nice view.

I started in the office, sitting at his desk I tried the drawers. Most had nothing of interest, a few chips, writing material and little else, though the bottom drawer had a bottle of fine whiskey. Too bad it would go to waste. I bagged the chips – just in case. A common hiding place, I ran my hand along the underside of the center drawer and felt something. A I pulled the drawer from the desk and turned it over. There, attached to the bottom was a chip, by the looks of it a low-capacity memory chip. I removed it and bagged it.

I fired up the computer but after I gained access (don't ask me how, it's a police secret) I searched it thoroughly, with ALURA's help. She found nothing of interest. No names at all in the contact list. The rest of the apt revealed nothing else of interest, other than that he had good taste in clothes and books. He actually had quite a collection of *real* bound books. Physical books are rare. I wondered how he could afford them on his salary.

Before I left, I looked in the bedroom. There wasn't much there except a weight lifting set and by

Stories My Mother Never Told Me

my uneducated count, some of the weights were missing – about thirty pounds worth. Out of habit I flashed them.

I left the apt and disposed of the key, it was single use anyway, and returned to my desk. There I fed the chip into my reader. Of course, the chip was protected but that never stopped me before. In a few seconds the chip was opened like one of Spence's books and I began to scan.

There wasn't a lot there, but what was, was very interesting indeed. Among other documents was a spreadsheet, the contents of which were quite incriminating. Had he been alive, Peter Spence would be in a world of hurt. The spreadsheet listed items by shipment date, the ship it arrived on, the departing ship, if any, its destination, the description, number of pieces, the value and the exact location in the warehouse. It was interesting how many items on the list were stored in the blue sector of the warehouse. Had he arranged that?

There was one last column that had check marks for most of the items. The descriptions, for the most part, were not very revealing; numbers,

Stories My Mother Never Told Me

abbreviations and the like but near the bottom was one item that I recognized. The full record read:

Date	2701.16.5.2
Ship In	Cloud Ranger
Ship Out	Star Wind
Dest.	Bells World
Desc.	Neuro TRX MET (MICETD) TX5056B74281
Qty.	5
Val.	100,000□ ea
Loc.	B3-7-4

"ALURA, where is the ship Star Wind? Is it still in port?"

"The ship Star Wind left port a week ago. It's halfway to the closest Chalmers by now."

Well, it couldn't be called back anyway. "Can we locate a copy of its manifest?" I asked.

Stories My Mother Never Told Me

"Just a moment while I retrieve it. I have it right here."

"Can you find the neuro device in it?"

Yes, Neuro TRX MET (MICETD) TX5056B74281 is listed as having passed customs as it was loaded onto the ship."

To pass customs a container has to be sealed. If the seal is broken the container is normally held until the contents can be fully accounted for. Then it receives a special seal indicating that customs has opened and examined the container. According to the manifest, this was not the case. But I had the feeling that someone on Bells World would be surprised to find a certain missing item, or five of them, that is.

So, what happened? Did Spence steal the implants with the intention of selling them or did someone pay him to do it? And did that someone kill him for it rather than pay a probably steep price. And one last question; was this a hobby of Spence's, stealing items in transit?

So many questions, so few answers. My biggest question is who was he in contact with and

Stories My Mother Never Told Me

did that individual contact Spence or did Spence contact him – or is it her? I scanned the small handful of other chips but they contained nothing important, a few games and little else.

Investigations are often a state of stop and go. Right now, I was nearly at a stop. Video surveillance might be of help.

"ALURA, will you review the warehouse surveillance videos for last Friday to see what kind of activity Mr. Spence might have been up to, assuming that the was there?"

"I'm on it," she replied.

"And I'm outta here," I said. It had been a long day and I was ready to pack it in. "Save the results of your search until tomorrow."

So, I went to my apt and brooded all through my cocktail and supper. I knew very little but of what I did know, something wasn't right. Something was ticking in the back of my mind like a word that is on the tip of your tongue. It was there, I could almost feel it and it kept rising close to the surface but just as I was ready to grab it, it would sink back into the depths of my mind. Like a tune you get into

Stories My Mother Never Told Me

your head, it would drive me crazy until I could get it. My best hope was that it would be there within range in the morning.

But when I woke it wasn't there and it quickly became a bothersome brain worm, oozing around back there unwilling to come to the light of day. So, I returned to my desk.

"ALURA, what did you find in the video? Anything interesting?"

"I did find something interesting. Last Friday Mr. Spense went to aisle 3 section 7 shelf 4. Does B3-7-4 ring a bell?"

I hated it when ALURA asked *me* questions, that was my job! But this time I had an answer, "Yes, that's the location the Neuro devices were stored. Can you show me?"

Almost immediately a HOLO rose from my desk and I watched Mr. Peter Spence go directly to that particular shelf. He took the package and replaced it with what looked identical to it. "Freeze that and zoom in to his hand and the package."

ALURA did so and I could clearly see the markings on the item as well as the intact seal.

Stories My Mother Never Told Me

Physical seals can't be hacked and if they show signs of tampering it is an immediate sign of foul play. No one would give this package a second glance. I wondered what was in it. Surely it wasn't any neural devices that *I* knew of.

The package, itself, was small and could be easily concealed but Spence openly carried it back to his post. There he casually placed it in a drawer and that was that.

"What else do you have?" I asked. The Holo didn't change but the timestamp did. Two hours later, Spence took the package from the drawer and walked through the warehouse to the western end. There he unlocked a door and went through it. The Holo jumped to show him entering a long hallway. There he walked a few feet, reached up and placed the package behind a ceiling tile. He did all of this so casually, I gained the impression that the surveillance vids weren't ever reviewed. It must have been assumed that security was very tight.

"Watch, there's more," said ALURA.

And there was. The timestamp jumped again by a few minutes and I watched Spence leave his

Stories My Mother Never Told Me

post and exit the warehouse by going through the administrative office.

"I followed him back to his apt. I also watched the hallway but nobody else entered it." ALURA said.

"So, is that it?"

"No, keep watching." I did and the scene jumped as did the timestamp. At 9:00 Friday evening I watched Spence walk down the hall from a distant point far to the north. He came to the hiding place and retrieved the package and then retraced his steps. The scene shifted to the Plaza and I saw him emerge from an alcove. The scene shifted again to a few seconds later as he approached the Bazaar. Again, the scene jumped to a vantage point within the Bazaar itself where I watched him melt into the Friday night crowd.

"That's where I lost him. I looked but he isn't seen on any camera after that."

"Damn, it's interesting but it doesn't get us any closer to his murder."

ALURA said, "I also did a thorough search for lifting weights but I didn't find anything."

Stories My Mother Never Told Me

That's when it hit me! Lifting weights. There were thirty pounds of them attached to Spence's body when he was brought up. I found a weight set in his apt and made the guess that thirty pounds were missing. That's what was in the back of my mind. Was Spence weighed down with his own weights? If he was, how were they transported to the reservoir in the first place? Did he carry them there? That seemed to be a very odd thing to do. Was he even alive at that point.

But if he was killed in his apt, which was a real possibility, it was a good mile, or more, to the reservoir. Did the murderer carry him and the weights all that way? Surely someone would have noticed.

"ALURA, scour the vids around Spence's apt from about 6:00pm on Friday until you find anything interesting. You know what to look for. I'm going for a walk."

My first destination was the ME's office. Bill was there and he showed me the weights. I looked at the flash photo that I had taken in his apt bedroom. The weights matched! One piece finally in place. I

Stories My Mother Never Told Me

hoped there were more to come. I thanked Bill and left.

I had a good idea of where Spence came to the surface, so to speak, when he exited the alcove near the Bazaar that I watched in the Holo. I wanted to see that place and see if I could get into the corridor at the rear of the warehouse.

It wasn't very far, actually, and I walked it in a few minutes. To the south of the hotel, which is right across the Plaza from the Bazaar, there is a maintenance alcove and that's where I suspected Spence to have exited. I entered the alcove and found a door. I used my universal key and the door easily opened. Inside there was a room with doors on either side and one in the rear. I made a guess and unlocked the one in the rear. Sure enough it led to a ramp, which I took all the way down to its end and stepped out into the long hallway that was behind the warehouse itself. It was the very hallway that Spence had used the previous Friday.

There was more than one door on the left side of the hallway. They could only have led into the warehouse itself. I guessed that each one entered the warehouse close to the center of a specifically colored area. There were a few doors along the right side of the hall as well. I opened the nearest one and found nothing more than a closet with supplies and a cleaning robot. I felt that I had wasted my time, so I backtracked to the entrance and crossed the Plaza to the Bazaar.

"ALURA, follow me and direct me to the last point where we have Spence on the vids. And how long until they're over written?"

"Most of them have already been overwritten. You should have put a hold on them."

Damn, another trail lost. "Keep what you already have."

The Bazaar is a large, and to some, a confusing place. It is easy to get lost. On the Plaza side the booths, studios and eateries are all open, well organized and clean. The "streets" are wide and easy to navigate. They also have names. But the deeper you get into the Bazaar the darker, more cramped and not as easy to navigate they become. Here the deals can get rather shady. It was these places that I believe Spence went to visit that Friday night.

Stories My Mother Never Told Me

ALURA guided me deep into the maze of "streets" in the Bazaar to a point where she said that the trail had been lost. I looked around and could see why. The light was dim and it looked like there were a number of places where it was possible to buy anything from a drink to a new kidney. I kid you not. It was the perfect place for Spence to unload his stolen property. But as I looked around, I wondered where to start.

I shrugged my shoulders and walked to the nearest bar. It was literally a bar, right on the "street." I ambled up and leaned on the fairly clean surface. The barkeep came over and asked, "What'll you have?"

"Any chance you were working here last Friday evening around 8:00?"

"I was here all night. I'm here every night."

I showed him a photo of Spence. "Any chance you saw this guy here that night?"

"Who's asking?"

I showed him my badge, "Will this help you remember?"

Stories My Mother Never Told Me

"Yeah, I seen him. He was here and had a drink. After a little while another guy came up, they talked and left."

Bingo! Success at the first try. Sometimes even I get lucky. "What did the other guy look like?"

"Just a regular guy, maybe five eight, brown hair."

That wasn't a lot to go on but it was something. "Did you see where they went?"

"Yeah, out towards the Plaza."

I thanked him and left. It *looked* like progress but I was getting nowhere fast. What did I know? A guy stole something relatively valuable, he got murdered and was sunk with his own lifting weights in the reservoir. Not much to go on. I left the Bazaar and headed for the Plaza where I could sit and think.

"ALURA, any chance that you got some vid of them leaving the Bazaar?"

"I may have gotten just a glimpse, only a couple of frames."

I sat at a table. "Show them to me."

Stories My Mother Never Told Me

Up popped the Holo and I could see two men leaving the Bazaar. Spence was easy to recognize but the other man was a mystery. "Can you identify the other man?"

"No. His face isn't in any database I have access to. My guess is that he must be an itinerant spacer."

"*My* guess is that you are wrong. His face may not be in any database, but I think he is a regular in this port. He didn't just stumble upon Spence. They must have known each other for a while. I have the feeling that our Mr. Spence was providing this guy with interesting things for quite a while. Of course, there's no way to prove it unless we actually capture this guy and my next guess is that he probably lifted off last Saturday. So can you tell me which ships left then?"

"Three ships lifted off last Saturday. They were the Space Witch, Nebula Rosa and Rim Runner."

"And where are they bound?"

"Space Witch is headed for Salda Minor, Nebula Rosa for Karnaugh and Rim Runner is

Stories My Mother Never Told Me

bound for the other side, out to the Rim worlds themselves."

"With a ship by that name and destination, I'm not surprised. I'll bet that Mr. Spence's mysterious friend is on that ship. Is there any chance that you can find even a frame of vid for when that ship was boarding?"

"Now you're pushing it."

"Look anyway, please."

After a few minutes she said, "Nothing. Sorry."

"Can you find a roster of the ship's crew and are there any photos?"

"Now you're really pushing it." There was another even longer wait. "Sorry, you're totally out of luck."

I knew that I was pushing it but I had to try. No matter how I looked at it, this case was back to square one. I've solved the case but I don't have a resolution. I know what was stolen and who took it. I don't know who the murderer is, I suspect strongly that he has the neuro devices, and I know where he's

Stories My Mother Never Told Me

going and that's at least four jumps away and about one hundred lights. And something told me that we'd never see him again. He'd killed his supplier and so there was no point in in him returning.

I'd have to tie up a few loose ends and write up my report, such as it was.

What a strange ending.

Part IV
The Perfect Crime

Now that I'm safely off planet, I can relax. After this trip, I don't think that I'm coming back. After all, Spence is dead and I have no other contacts. Besides which, they probably have vids or photos of me and will be looking for me in the future, so I'm outa there – for good. Once I sell those Neuros, I'll be set for a very long time. I've got five of them and I should get more than six figures for the lot.

I've bounced around this part of the cluster for many years, so it is a natural time to move on. My crimes are many, though mostly smuggling. Pete Spence was my most valuable contact. It seems that

Stories My Mother Never Told Me

he could get almost anything I asked for and a few times he offered things that I wasn't even looking for. A good example is these Neuros.

As soon as me mentioned them to me, I knew that I cold unload them out on the Rim for a good hunk of money. I also knew that it would be dangerous if word leaked out that they were missing. I knew that Spence could be trusted but I also knew that things were tightening up with customs. Bringing things in and out hasn't been as easy as it used to be. But Spence had it covered.

So why kill him? For a start it was strictly business. I had no animosity against him, I just knew, from the beginning of this job that he had to go. After he told me about the Neuros and offered them to me, it was a done deal. All I had to do was make my plans in detail and follow through to the letter. If I did that, I'd have the Neuros for free but, in the process, he had to die. I couldn't afford to have him hunting for me. He was as efficient as I am and there was no doubt that he would find me.

I had been in Thevenin for a couple of months and had made contact with him early on but he didn't have anything and there was nothing I was

Stories My Mother Never Told Me

looking for, so I bounced around trying to latch onto something that would be profitable.

It was something of a surprise when he contacted me. We met in our usual place in the Bazaar, talking as we wandered through the maze of studios, shops and bars.

"I have something you have never seen and I'm willing to part with, at a reasonable price."

"What is it and how much?"

"Well," Spence said, "I don't have it yet, but it is coming in next week. It will pass through the warehouse and I can ensure that it will park in my sector. I'm not sure yet, but I expect to have it in my possession for about a week."

"So, what is it?" I asked.

"Ever hear of a Neuro TRX MET Implant?"

"Can't say that I have. What *is* it?"

"It's a neuro transmitter that is implanted in the human body. It's used to control various nervous system functions. Mostly pain, uncontrollable muscle spasms and the like. It's programmable for whatever it is needed to do."

Stories My Mother Never Told Me

"And why am I interested in something like that?"

"Because," he said. "This thing is easily hacked and can be implanted in the brain stem and give the user the most intense pleasure imaginable. Better than sex! So much so that it creates an addiction on the first use. There are people out there who would pay a high premium for something like that. And I'll have five of them next week. You could probably unload the lot for well over a million out in the Rim and I'm asking far less than that."

"Isn't something like that traceable?"

"I've got that covered," Spence told me. I'll replicate the packaging so well that customs won't pay a second glance at the fake when it goes out. Guaranteed. And when the switch is discovered, it will be too late to trace."

"So how much do you want?"

"Two hundred fifty, up front."

I rubbed my jaw, "That's a lot of dough. I gotta look around to see what I can shake loose."

Stories My Mother Never Told Me

"You have a week. I'll be in touch when they come in."

That gave me some time to do some research to see if these things were real. I discovered that implants of this type, but much more primitive, had been around for hundreds of years. But these were so much more sophisticated. They are programmable for the specific part of the body as well as the application required. As a result, they can easily be hacked to do things that they are not designed to do. By stimulating the pleasure centers of the brain, they are almost immediately addictive and overuse can actually result in the death of the user. Interestingly, they can be removed and reimplanted in another victim – er person.

This sounded exactly like something that I could traffic in the Rim and make a handsome profit. Of course, there was no way that I could raise that kind of money to pay Spence, but I didn't worry about that. I have no scruples, so I figured that I wouldn't have to pay. Of course, Pete Spence didn't know that – and he didn't have to. In fact, he'd never find out.

Stories My Mother Never Told Me

Now I'm not a cruel man, but sometimes things just have to be done. But before that could happen, I had to have a plan, a complete plan, one from A, get the loot, to Z, dispose of the body.

Oh, you're surprised? What did you think I was contemplating? Shaking his hand and saying 'thank you?'

Mr. Spence had just about filled his card anyway. After this I didn't contemplate doing any more business with him and I'm not one to take chances. Suppose his ruse, whatever it was, wouldn't get past customs. If he got caught, would he keep his mouth shut? It was a chance I simply couldn't afford to take, so I wouldn't.

So, I had to make careful and clear plans for every step of the operation. I set to work, making my plans. My first task was how and where to dispose of the body. I've always felt that it's best to work backwards.

Over the years Spence and I had passed goods in many different places in the spaceport and never the same place twice. I remembered the one time we made our transaction in the reservoir. It was a secure place and was almost always empty. No one

Stories My Mother Never Told Me

had any real reason to be there but it was accessible so that maintenance could be done. That sounded to me like a good place to stash a body. Might even take a while to be found.

That out of the way I had to figure how to get the limp Mr. Spence from his apt, yes that's where I planned to do the deed, to the reservoir. There were plenty of options. Obviously, I couldn't carry him but a manual wheelchair wasn't out of the question. There had to be a number of places where one could be borrowed, or stolen.

So, it all began to fall in place. Now all I had to do was wait, And, it was a long week. But I made good use of my time. I learned the path from his apt, via the Slider, to the entrance of the reservoir. I scouted out places for wheelchairs. Rope would be easy to come by, especially if I could steal about ten feet. I knew places in the field where that could be found.

I bided my time for a week. And finally, the call came.

"I got our stuff. We can make the exchange at your convenience. Where do you want to meet?"

Stories My Mother Never Told Me

I couldn't very well say, 'your place,' so I said, "The Bazaar?"

"Tomorrow at 9:00pm. Be there."

I said I would. And I was. It looked like it would throw a major wrench into my plans but I had to play it by ear. We met at the Bazaar and walked our usual route. We stopped at one of the bars and had a drink. So far, the subject of our meeting hadn't been raised. As we left the bar, fortified, I said, "So where's the loot? When can I see these Neuros?"

"You have the money?"

"Of course, I do, but I'm not going to flash it, especially here. I won't bring it out until I see the stuff. So how about it?"

Glory of glories he said, "It's at my place. It's too hot to bring out here. We'll go back to my place and make the trade."

"Let's go," I said.

So, we took the Slider back to his apt and he let us in. We stood in his living room. "Wait here while I get it." And he left the room. I looked out the

Stories My Mother Never Told Me

HoloWall at the forest of course, there's not much to see at night. But I didn't have long to wait.

Spence brought out a package and placed it on the kitchen table. He pointed at it and I took out my vibroblade and cut the package open. I really didn't know what I was looking at but it looked right. There was even a documentation and programming chip with the set. While I examined the package Spence stood looking through the HoloWall.

I quickly stepped up to him and put my left arm around him and slammed the vibroblade hilt into his upper back. I hit the release and felt the tingle as the blade came into being. Almost immediately he slumped and he was dead before he hit the floor.

I like vibroblades because they are silent and clean. His clothes and even his skin was not cut. No blood. The damage was done only inside the body, leaving no trace, that is until the post mortem. And I wasn't going to leave his body lying around here waiting for someone to call. No, he had to take a swim.

I left him lying there while I rummaged through the apt looking for whatever I could use to

Stories My Mother Never Told Me

truss him up. I hadn't thought about weights, but should have. The best laid plans and all that. But again, I got lucky. There in the bedroom was a weight lifting set and there were a number of disc weights. They would do nicely. I already had some rope that I had taken from a pile in the field, so that was taken care of. All I needed was the wheelchair. I knew that most residential buildings had wheelchairs for occasional use by the residents, so surely there would be one around somewhere.

I left the apt and went to the ground floor and looked in the storage room. My incredible luck held and I found one in the corner. Within moments I was wheeling it into the jump tube and up to Spence's apt. There I wheeled into the living room and set to work.

I wrestled his very limp and unhelpful body into the chair and got it into a fairly presentable position. I tied him into a sitting position and put the weights in his lap. He should look fairly natural in the dimness of the night. I rummaged through his pockets until I found his pass cards. One of them would open the reservoir door. With only three cards it should be easy.

Stories My Mother Never Told Me

All things being ready I thumbed the door and wheeled him out into the hallway and to the jump tube. The ride down wasn't bad, though I had a little concern that the chair would give me problems, but it didn't. Once down the push to the Slider was only a couple of minutes. At this time of night there were very few people about. The ride to the opposite end was quick and easy.

The ramp at the other end led to the Plaza itself, just beyond the Bazaar parameter. I wheeled us along the walkway to an alcove near the end. I turned right, into it, and followed the short hallway to the end. There were two doors. I believed that the one on the left was the one I wanted.

Some things in Thevenin are much more accessible than they should be. The first card I tried worked and we passed through the open door. I wheeled Spences body down the ramp. The humid air told me that I had found the right place. I rolled the chair to the edge of the pool and put the weights on the floor. Then I pushed the body onto the concrete floor and rolled the wheelchair against the wall.

Stories My Mother Never Told Me

It only took a few moments to truss Spence's body and attach the weights to the arms, legs and torso. Then a quick roll and the satisfying splash as the late Mr. Spence entered his eternal rest – at least until they found him, which they surely would.

I took the chair and left. I didn't return the chair to the place I found it, I simply abandoned it at the entrance of the Bazaar, where there were two wheelchairs there already. Perfect.

The next morning, I boarded my ship, the Rim Runner and settled in for the long haul. It would be many months before we reached our destination. I had a lot of time to prepare for the sale of the Neuros.

And I had a lot of time to contemplate the perfect crime. That is - murder most rare.

Stories My Mother Never Told Me

So, we reach the end of this little volume. I hope mother would have approved of these stories. And, of course, I truly hope that you have not only approved but enjoyed them as well. And now, for the nonce, I'm off to other things.

Huntsville, Al
October 28, 2023